'This happens to be *my* flat.' His voice was dangerously soft. 'And now that we've established that my credentials are perfectly bona fide—I'll repeat my question and ask again what you're doing here?'

'I live here, too. Or rather I did from about one hour ago,' Louisa replied evenly. She gave him a superior smile. 'It seems that I'm not the only one to make assumptions, doesn't it? I am not a nurse, and I never have been.'

The turquoise eyes had narrowed and Adam was staring at her consideringly, comprehension beginning to dawn.

'You mean—that you're a doctor, too?'

'Ten out of ten for perception,' she replied sarcastically, pleased to see him at a disadvantage at last.

Sharon Wirdnam has been a waitress, a photographer and a cook. She then trained as a nurse and medical secretary and found that she enjoyed working in a caring environment. She decided that one day she would write about romance against the dramatic backdrop of hospital life.

She was encouraged to write by her doctor husband after the birth of their two children, and much of her medical information comes from him, and from friends. She lives in Surrey, where her husband is a GP.

Previous Titles

TO BREAK A DOCTOR'S HEART
NURSE IN THE OUTBACK

For Tony Kendrick

A MEDICAL LIAISON

BY

SHARON WIRDNAM

MILLS & BOON LIMITED
ETON HOUSE   18–24 PARADISE ROAD
RICHMOND   SURREY   TW9 1SR

First published in Great Britain 1990
by Mills & Boon Limited

© Sharon Wirdnam 1990

Australian copyright 1990
Philippine copyright 1990
This edition 1990

ISBN 0 263 76845 7

Set in 11 on 12½ pt Linotron Palatino
03-9006-44430
Typeset in Great Britain by Centracet, Cambridge
Made and printed in Great Britain

CHAPTER ONE

'HELL's bells!'

Louisa jammed the brakes on just in time to see the scrawny black and white cat narrowly miss the front bumper. Now she knew why cats had nine lives! She watched as it tore off towards the main building before she restarted the engine.

She eased the car into the nearest space, next to the notice which said 'Hospital—Staff Only', and reached up underneath the rather battered glove compartment to open the boot. The boot catch was released with a distinctive squeak and she smiled affectionately. She just seemed to go on forever, this little car. Left out on bitter frosty nights, she always started first time. Scrimped and saved for by Louisa as a student, time and again she had proved well worth the money she had cost.

Louisa sat there for a moment or two in silence, just collecting her thoughts as she stared at the impressive structure of St Dunstan's Hospital. It was an odd mishmash of buildings, many with monstrous time-blackened turrets. The main ward block was modern, though, its gleaming chrome and large plate-glass windows standing curiously at ease among its older counterparts.

As she watched in the gathering dusk, lights began to be flicked on, and she saw nurses scurrying from bed to bed with cups of late afternoon tea, a white-coated figure taking a stethoscope from his pocket, and a porter slowly pushing a trolley up the ward.

She sat very still, relishing her last few moments of anonymity—soon some of these people would be known to her—their foibles and their loyalties. She would be working alongside them, learning how this particular hospital did things. A new life, in a new hospital—far away from the tatters of her old one.

She was about to open her door when she noticed a movement in her rear mirror and she looked up and frowned, for a particularly expensive-looking car was flicking its headlights on and off, almost blinding her with its over-impressive array of illuminations.

She got out of her car slowly and turned towards the other vehicle, raising a rather resigned eyebrow. She couldn't help it—she knew it was blind prejudice, but she despised such ostentatious displays of wealth.

The driver was getting out—an impossibly tall man who she was surprised could fit into such a cramped little machine. And, on further examination, he didn't look in the least like the usual sports car owner. His cords were unpressed and his thick sweater had clearly seen better days. He looked as though he would be more at home behind the wheel of a Land Rover, she thought, noticing that he was now staring at her impatiently.

Returning his stare, she felt the jarring jolt of recognition—for she knew that craggy face, with its high cheekbones and narrow eyes. Yet she was positive that she had never met the man before in her life. Her memory was fault-less—she would never have forgotten meeting someone like him, if not because of his looks then for his glowering expression alone!

She shook her head a little—the long drive had affected her and now she was imagining things! The tall man in front of her was a complete stranger—of that she was certain.

'That's *my* space you're parking in,' he began, a frown creasing his forehead above dark brows.

She sighed. Men were always so predictably proprietorial about parking. If they left their wretched cars in the same spot for two days running it mysteriously became 'theirs', and the more expensive the car, the more arrogant the owner. She gazed up at him sweetly.

'Then I must either be blind or unobservant,' she answered calmly. 'Because I'm afraid I didn't notice a sign next to it marked "Reserved".'

Now it was his turn to raise his eyebrows, the composure of her reply making him look at her properly, as if for the first time.

She could see him taking in the pencil-slim

grey skirt which just skimmed her knees, with its matching, rather severe jacket. The sombre colour of the suit provided a fitting backdrop for the living colour of her thick dark hair with its chestnut highlights which swirled in glorious waves around her shoulders. She couldn't miss the brief flash of appreciation in his eyes, or the imperceptible change in his manner.

'It isn't actually reserved for me,' he said grudgingly. 'It's just that I've kind of ear-marked it for myself. You must be new here, or you probably would have noticed me using it before?'

The implication being that anyone who knew him wouldn't dare park in his spot, she thought with amusement. Well, he had picked the wrong person to challenge in her. If the last few years had taught her anything, it was that never again would she allow herself to be intimidated.

'Yes, I'm new here,' she agreed politely, pull-ing open the boot and removing her only suitcase.

He appeared to be waiting for something.

'Well? Aren't you going to move it?' he demanded.

She opened her eyes very wide. 'Don't be so absurd! There are dozens of other places you can park in, and anyway—I can't guarantee that my car will start again. It's a very old car!'

That was supposed to be a joke, she thought, as she met his unsmiling eyes. She wondered whose bed he'd got out the wrong side of that morning!

He gave her a final glare before turning away, but at least she might as well get some directions out of him.

'Excuse me,' she called after him. 'I'm looking for——'

'The tall building directly to your left,' he interrupted rudely.

'Pardon?'

'The Nurses' Home.' He pointed as he walked away. 'It's over there.'

She almost laughed aloud as she locked the door, popping the key into a slim black leather clutchbag. She had long stopped being offended when people mistook her for a nurse, even if they did think that she was an unqualified one! It was a common enough mistake in an institution where seventy-five per cent of the females were indeed nurses. And perhaps it had something to do with her smallness, or the kittenish appeal of her looks, which made it hard for people to believe that she was not a nineteen-year-old nurse, but in fact a qualified doctor of almost twenty-five!

She guessed that he was a doctor, too. He had the same kind of careless arrogance which she had encountered often enough among the male members of the profession. She had been reluctant to disclose that she was a member of the same profession, and see the speculative look change to one of wariness as he acknowledged an equal, rather than a subordinate.

As she watched him disappear into the distance she decided to seek directions from someone else—someone with less of an axe to grind!

She soon found a porter who insisted on carrying her suitcase to the Doctors' Residence for her.

Inside the building she took the lift to the fifth floor and peered at the numbers on the doors in the dimly lit corridor until she found flat fourteen. She had been told that she would be sharing with another doctor, but there was no sign of life as she let herself in and thankfully dumped her case in the hall.

Her own room was immediately to the left of the front door and marked 'Dr L. Grey' and she sighed as she noted that they had spelt her name incorrectly. She pulled the card out, intending to change it later, and took the suitcase into her new abode.

The room was small, but perfectly adequate for her needs with a single bed and locker, a bookcase and a narrow desk with an Anglepoise lamp on it, which she would be using a great deal. She intended to be successful in her chosen profession, and to be successful meant lots of hard work.

She quickly unpacked her clothes, her shoes and toiletries, and lined the few textbooks she possessed neatly in the bookcase. When she had finished and closed the wardrobe door, the room looked scarcely different than it had when she had first set foot inside it. The photo of her Aunt Beatrice in its silver frame added the one personal touch. She had once cared passionately about her surroundings, but no more. Mentally and physically she liked to travel light.

The other occupant of the flat seemed to share few of the same characteristics—the sitting-room was a conglomeration of messy disarray, with bright cushions spilling from the sofa on to the floor, and magazines and newspapers jostling for space on the coffee-table. The kitchen looked as though someone had attempted to start World War III in there—two empty wine glasses and an almost empty bottle of Chianti were lined up on a cluttered draining-board, where a pan lightly covered with hardening strands of spaghetti stood next to a saucepan of congealed bolognese sauce.

The general air of chaos reminded Louisa of Megan, her scatty ex-flatmate—the two girls had shared a flat for several years, and Louisa was going to miss her.

She automatically squirted some washing-up liquid into the bowl, filled it with hot water, and began washing the glasses and plates methodically. Glasses first, cups second, plates and crockery next, then pans. Strange how so many of her peers despised housework, she reflected as she rinsed the suds off one of the glasses and placed it carefully on the draining-board. She wouldn't go so far as to say that she actually *loved* washing-up and cleaning, but she found the repetition and the mindlessness of it curiously relaxing. And it was in such contrast to the taxing mental nature of her job.

Not that she would ever have dared admit it to anyone, she thought delightedly as she pulled the plug out and dreamily watched the water begin to drain away. The image of career girl and *hausfrau* did not exactly marry very well together!

She heard the front door slam and footsteps stop as their owner must have paused to notice the light on in the kitchen. She turned around with a welcoming expression as she heard a sound behind her, the smile quickly changing to a gape of astonishment as she found herself staring at a very tall, newly familiar man. It was the driver of the Porsche!

He stood, hands on his hips, his eyes glancing over to the just washed plates and then back again, his height seeming to fill the small kitchen. She had never felt so unwelcome in her entire life.

'What the hell are you doing in here?' he demanded in disbelief, looking at her as though she had broken into the place.

'You've got eyes in your head, haven't you?' she snapped back at him. 'What do you think I'm doing? It's called washing-up!'

There was something about him which was making all her hackles rise. It wasn't just his earlier rudeness or the way he was regarding her, although that was irritating enough. It went much deeper than that. It was something about being at such close quarters to a man again— and a man who seemed to exude such a raw masculine sensuality from every pore—which made her want to run away from him. As if his very proximity could do her harm.

'And anyway——' she stuck her small chin out belligerently '—I'd like to know what you're doing here, if it comes to that.'

A look of intense irritation flashed across his face. 'I'll give you three guesses,' he said silkily.

That was easy enough.

'I assume,' she replied tartly, her words measured, trying hard to keep the bitterness out of them, 'I assume that you are the boyfriend of the occupant of this flat, a contributor to the messy plates I've just cleared away, and that you have your own key to come and go as you please.' Something which will have to stop now that I'm here, she wanted to add—but didn't quite have the courage to do so.

They stood facing one another and she noticed for the first time what an unusual colour his eyes were—an extraordinary shade of icy turquoise—the colour of a swimming pool on a sunny day. Film star eyes. Again came the niggling thought that she was sure she knew his face.

His words, too, were measured, sounding like those of someone who was holding on to his temper with extreme difficulty. 'Then your assumption is incorrect.' His voice was dangerously soft. 'I am not the occupant's "boyfriend", to use your rather schoolgirlish vernacular—this happens to be *my* flat. Yes, indeed.' He had noticed her start. 'And now that we've established that my credentials are perfectly bona fide—I'll repeat my question and ask again what you're doing here?'

'I live here, too. Or rather I did from about one hour ago,' she replied evenly, her mind racing to try to grasp the situation.

Now it was his turn to look surprised.

'Don't be ridiculous! What are you talking about? You've obviously been given the wrong keys—you're a nurse, for goodness' sake!'

She gave him a superior smile. 'It seems that I'm not the only one to make assumptions, doesn't it? I am not a nurse, and I never have been.'

'But you said——'

'I said *nothing*,' she interrupted coldly. 'I agreed that I was new here and you took that to mean that I was a nurse. Presumably,' she added, 'because I'm female.'

The turquoise eyes had narrowed and he was staring at her consideringly, comprehension beginning to dawn.

'You mean—that you're a doctor, too?'

'Ten out of ten for perception,' she replied sarcastically, pleased to see him at a disadvantage at last.

He didn't remain at a disadvantage for long,

however; he glowered at her and marched out of the kitchen into the hall, where she heard him pick up a telephone. She followed in his wake slowly, drying her hands on the tea-towel, amused to hear what would now transpire.

He glanced up at her briefly, then away, ignoring her completely.

'Mrs Jefferson, please,' he said shortly into the receiver. There was a pause. 'Adam Forrester.'

She looked up in surprise. So that was it! No wonder she had thought she had known him—who, both in and outside the medical profession, hadn't heard of Dr Adam Forrester?

He'd been considered a prodigy, mainly because he'd written a book while still at medical school which had become required reading for all students—she'd read it herself.

But it had been work done during research for his thesis which had aroused the interest of the general public. He had fed some laboratory mice some of his watercress salad and had discovered that it had made them sexually more active. The tabloid press had had a field-day—the *News of the World* had run a full-page story with banner headlines claiming 'Doc says watercress makes you sexy!' Watercress sales had soared; he had been invited on to a chat show and had proved so popular that a television series had followed.

Here's Health had run for almost two years, a popular and light-hearted Sunday evening show—and then it had suddenly stopped, at the height of its popularity, and Adam Forrester had disappeared from view.

Louisa surreptitiously glanced around the walls of the hall they stood in. What on earth was he doing living in a place like this? It was bright enough, with pale magnolia walls, but they were bare of adornment. It was just not the kind of place you imagined a wealthy and successful doctor living—he looked to be in his mid-thirties, so why wasn't he residing in some stone-built mansion in the countryside?

'I don't care that it's Sunday evening,' he was saying. 'I need to speak to her now.'

It was the kind of tone which did not invite argument, and she could just imagine a flummoxed telephonist agreeing to his request.

He looked up again. 'There's no need for you to hang around,' he told her. 'I can sort this out.'

'Oh, but I'd like to listen,' she said sweetly. 'If that's all right with you?'

Clearly, it was not all right with him, but as he couldn't actually eject her physically, especially while talking into the phone, he was forced to content himself with an exaggeratedly loud sigh.

After a couple of minutes of silence he was connected.

'Mrs Jefferson?' he barked. 'It's Adam Forrester here.' He listened for a moment. 'Yes, of course I realise it's a Sunday evening,' he exploded. 'And if you're trying to make a point about being disturbed, don't bother—it's about time you administrators sorted out a legitimate problem, instead of trying to disrupt the running of the wards!'

Louisa could hear an indignant reply.

'I'd like to know just why I happen to have a *woman* doctor sharing my flat with me?' He spat the word out as though it were poison.

The expression on his face as he listened to the reply was almost comical.

'I see,' he said coldly. 'I must say that I have never heard such a load of pretentious old claptrap in my life!' He glanced at his watch. 'Perhaps it *is* too late to do anything about it this evening, but you can be sure that first thing in the morning—I want this thing sorted out!'

He slammed the receiver back into its hook, so that the whole phone shook, and turned to face Louisa.

'It seems,' he said heavily, 'that some of your more eloquent predecessors are responsible for your being here.'

'What are you talking about?'

'I'm talking about a group of female doctors who took it upon themselves to complain about being given flats in the Nurses' Home, on the grounds of sexual discrimination. When it was pointed out to them that this might mean sharing flats with the male doctors—they apparently replied that this was how it should be. That they were not helpless maidens who needed protecting, and did not expect to be treated any differently from their male counterparts. Typical!' he finished disgustedly.

There was a short tussle as loyalty to this radical group of females struggled to overcome the natural abhorrence she felt at living in such close quarters to a man again. And not just any man. *This* man! But it would simply remove any dignity she had to get into an argument with him about it. He was right, it could all be sorted out in the morning.

'Don't worry, Dr Forrester,' she said haughtily. 'I find the situation as unappealing as you obviously do. But no doubt I can tolerate it for one night.'

'I suppose so,' he grunted. His eyes swept over her assessingly again, as they had done in the car park, and there was something about the look which made her feel totally exposed and vulnerable.

She met his eyes defiantly, determined that he should not see how much his presence disturbed her.

'I usually take a shower around ten. So you'd better scurry back to your room by then. Unless——' he grinned for the first time, a roguish grin which left her in no doubt whatsoever as to his thoughts '—unless,' he continued, 'you'd care to appreciate the delights of my naked body?'

She knew that his words were mocking, but

she flushed scarlet, mentally trying to block out the images which came rushing into her mind at his words.

'Not if I want my stomach to retain its contents!' she snapped, hoping that the sharp words would detract from her discomposure.

She made as if to leave, but he caught her arm, the turquoise-blue eyes boring holes into her. 'Oh, don't worry,' he whispered, emphasising each word as if to impress its meaning on her. 'I never play this close to home.'

He released her arm. 'By the way—do you realise that I still don't even know your name?'

She angrily pushed a thick wave of chestnut hair back from her face. 'And you don't need to either. After tonight, Dr Forrester—I hope I never set eyes on you again!'

She would have loved to have stabbed the heel of her neat black court shoe into his ankle, but she contented herself with a final glower before walking back to her room and slamming the door shut very loudly behind her.

CHAPTER TWO

LOUISA stood in the centre of the room, still breathing heavily in anger, looking at the surroundings which such a short time ago had been her 'home', but which she would now almost certainly be moving out of.

What a start! And what a man! She remembered how tranquil her thoughts had been in the car this afternoon, on the long drive up from London, anticipating her first job as a qualified doctor. And now this. Not the most auspicious of beginnings.

She walked over to her desk and tapped her fingers restlessly over a medical textbook. What was it the Dean had said about her as he had handed her the coveted Bailey prize for biochemistry in her third year? That she was calm, and unflappable, and dedicated. Oh, and ambitious. She mustn't forget the bit about ambition—Mike would certainly be disappointed if she left that bit out. It was a quality which was lauded if possessed by a man, yet seemed to be greatly despised in a woman.

Men. They stood in your way and they got under your skin with their demands for more time, more meals, more of everything, until you had precious little left for yourself.

She had come to St Dunstan's to forget men and to begin a new life in her chosen field of medicine. She had set herself various goals, and one of them was to start work for her MRCP examination as soon as she possibly could. Membership of the Royal College of Physicians was essential if one planned to make a career in hospital medicine. It was a tough exam, and the pass rate was low, but Louisa was determined to pass first time.

She switched on the Anglepoise lamp and sat down at the desk. She was going to have to work very hard indeed to get on—women in medicine didn't have to be *as* good as their male counterparts, they had to be better. She had heard from older women doctors that even when you did land a good job, there were often the snide comments, that you'd fluttered your eyelashes in the right direction, flirted with the boss. Prejudice was alive and well in the 1990s!

She opened up the textbook, chuckling gently to herself as she did so. She could just imagine the smouldering resentment which must have led a group of her peers to campaign for sexual equality in the matter of accommodation—what a brave lot they must have been! Not that she had anything personally to thank them for— they were partly responsible for her having blushed for the first time in years.

Never mind, even if he had noticed her pink cheeks, it would be of little account in the morning. He could think what he jolly well liked.

Opening up the colossal tome which lay before her, she found the page on 'Cardiological disorders in young adults', and after a few moments was thinking of nothing else.

She came to with a start and, glancing down at her watch, realised that she had been reading for almost two and a half hours. Almost a quarter to nine. She was willing to bet that the canteen would have shut by now and she hadn't brought any provisions with her.

As if in protest at her thoughts, her stomach gave a loud rumble. Lunch had been a hurried sandwich and a coffee in a motorway service station. Naturally slim, never having to diet, she could not, however, imagine surviving without anything more to eat until the morning.

So she had but two options—she could either wander around this unfamiliar hospital in the dark in search of a meal which she could not even guarantee being able to get at this time of night. Or she could be sensible and ask Adam Forrester to loan her something until the morning.

So why did she recoil from the most sensible option? Was it because Dr Forrester had already had the most strange effect on her normally unruffable composure?

She stood up, stretching slowly. It was of no matter—she would do the most practical thing and go and ask him.

She caught sight of herself in the mirror as she clicked off the desk lamp. She had stupidly sat down to study in her grey suit, and the narrow skirt looked crumpled. It would need pressing before she could wear it for work.

She pulled the jacket and the skirt off, and the white silky shirt which she wore underneath—and pulled a pair of old jeans from out of the drawer. Some colours were difficult to wear with her pale skin, but the jade-green angora sweater she pulled over the dark red hair suited her perfectly, while the casual clothes had the effect of making her appear even younger, and much softer.

She let herself quietly out of her room, listening out for him, but the sitting-room and the kitchen were empty. She could see light shining from the crack underneath his door and so, rather reluctantly, she raised her fist and tapped twice.

There was no reply and it occurred to her that he might actually be ignoring her—but surely he wouldn't be so childish? She raised her hand to knock for the last time when the door was flung open and he stood there, staring down at her with what looked like his habitual impatient expression.

He too had changed into jeans, and had removed the thick jumper he'd been wearing—instead he had on a thin shirt, unbuttoned at the neck and showing a great deal of very dark hair on his chest. And his feet were bare. She found herself staring at them.

'Yes? What is it?' he demanded perfunctorily.

There was nothing of his earlier manner about him now, his attitude was brisk and business-like, almost as if they had never spoken before.

'I'm afraid I've been working and didn't real-ise it had got so late,' she began, attempting to give him a pleasant smile.

'Get to the point, will you?'

She bit back an angry retort to his rudeness— she was, after all, asking him a favour!

'I'm very hungry, and think I must have missed the canteen—and wondered if you'd lend me something to eat? I could repay you tomorrow.'

There was something so very un-English about asking for favours, particularly from a comparative stranger, she thought, interpreting his frown as one of irritation at her request.

He looked at his watch. 'Yes, you will have missed supper.'

Behind him she could see into his room—a replica of her own—but it shared none of the untidiness of the sitting-room she had seen earlier. She wondered who he had been sharing a meal with.

She could see everything neatly arranged, the bed smooth, books in neat lines on the shelves, and, judging from the light at his desk and the open books, he too had been studying.

'There isn't anything very much,' he said

ungraciously. 'I was planning to make myself an omelette—you're welcome to share that if you like.'

She had definitely not anticipated dining with him, but she couldn't really insist on taking his food and then eating it in the privacy of her own room!

Instead she nodded. 'An omelette will be fine, thanks.'

She stood there for a moment hesitantly, and he must have taken the hint because he closed his door and led the way through into the kitchen.

'Do you want me to do anything?' she asked.

'I think I can just about manage an omelette,' he said sarcastically.

What a bad-tempered man he was, she thought as she sat down at the kitchen table, tucking her slim legs underneath. She would much rather he had given her the eggs and she could have cooked for herself after he had finished. It seemed a bit of a farce to eat a meal together when he obviously couldn't stand the sight of her.

She watched as he cracked the eggs into a glass bowl, and beat them with milk and salt and pepper.

'Cheese OK for you?'

She nodded. 'Thanks.'

He was certainly very organised—he melted butter in the pan and swirled the mixture on to it like a past master of the art, even browning the omelette under the grill so that it puffed up to twice its size.

When he placed the plate before her she smiled up at him—however crotchety he was, her stomach was certainly grateful!

He reached down into the bottom shelf of the fridge.

'Do you want a beer?'

In fact she rarely drank much at all, but the hassle of requesting a cup of coffee from someone so unforthcoming was too much to contemplate.

'Yes, please.'

He poured her out a glass of lager, and sitting down at the table opposite her, drank his own straight from the can. She sipped thirstily in between mouthfuls of omelette and brown bread.

She finished her meal to find that his own was scarcely touched, and he was regarding her with almost a glint of amusement in his eyes.

'Why, you've hardly eaten any of yours!' she exclaimed. 'Aren't you hungry?'

He actually smiled at her! 'Not as hungry as you were, obviously! Do you want something else? Yoghurt? Fruit?'

She finished off the last of her beer. 'No, thanks—that was plenty. I might just make a cup of coffee in the morning—if that's all right?'

He indicated a cupboard by the cooker. 'Sure. It's all in there. Help yourself.'

She stood up a little unsteadily; the glass of

unaccustomed alcohol on a virtually empty stomach had affected her more than it should have done.

She cleared her throat, and the icy turquoise eyes glanced at her questioningly.

'I'm sorry there's been this mix-up,' she babbled. 'I'll come and collect my things tomorrow, when they find me somewhere else.'

He gave her the faintest of smiles and she could have kicked herself—she hadn't meant it to sound as if she was apologising for being here. She paused in the doorway, the beer seeming to have given her an uncontrollable urge to talk.

'I don't expect you *are* very hungry.' She smiled, remembering the dishes she had washed up on her arrival. 'It looked a delicious bolognese sauce!'

What *had* she said to offend him? He looked absolutely furious. He stood up suddenly and stared at her as witheringly as if she had been some small mollusc on the floor in front of him.

'How like a woman,' he muttered in disgust. 'Even when there's nothing to say, she'll always come out with some meaningless babble. What is it they say about empty vessels?'

She stared at him, speechless for a moment. She had never in her life been spoken to in such a rude, dismissive manner by a virtual stranger. What God-given right did this man have to behave in such an unpleasant way?

She regarded him coldly, suddenly completely sober again.

'You seem to have a problem with communication, Dr Forrester. How surprising for someone who has worked so much in the media! You are rude and boorish. And a bully,' she added, thinking of how he had snapped so unnecessarily on the telephone. 'Personally, I'd get something done about it if I were you—it can't make you a very good doctor, now can it?'

She didn't bother to wait around for his reply, but she saw that her barb had definitely reached its target, for his face was as black as thunder.

The short walk back to her room seemed to last forever. It felt as though she was walking the plank. She didn't know what she was expecting him to do—rush after her and blast her out—but, in fact, he did nothing.

Once inside, she waited until she heard him go back to his room before she hurried in to use the bathroom. She bathed and brushed her teeth and wrapped her dressing-gown around her tightly before going back to her room, remembering his words and feeling stupidly afraid that perhaps she *might* come face to face with his naked body.

She read her book for a while longer, and decided to turn in for an early night before starting her new job—she wanted to be refreshed and rested to face all the hard work which lay ahead of her.

And then she did something she'd never done in all the time she'd lived away from home.

Turning the key in the door, she locked herself in.

CHAPTER THREE

LOUISA awoke with that curious feeling of disorientation which accompanied the first night spent in a strange bed. Even before she opened her eyes she seemed to sense the unfamiliar surroundings, and she came to slowly, seeing the pale light of the winter morning come creeping through the ghastly hospital curtains of orange and brown.

She sat up and clicked off the alarm clock she had not needed—she was so used to waking before seven that it had now become second nature to her. Her fears of the night before now served only to niggle her with an embarrassed shame. No doubt the women doctors who had fought for this particular equality would be appalled if they'd known that she had barricaded herself in her bedroom like some medieval virgin—but then, they had probably never met Adam Forrester!

Nevertheless, she sat still in bed for the moment, clad in one of the baggy T-shirts she always wore, listening out for any signs of life or, more specifically, any indication that the man himself might be roaming around the flat in his threatened lack of attire.

But she heard nothing, and so swung her legs

out of the bed, pulled on her dressing-gown
and headed for the bathroom with a youthful
exuberance which was hard to dispel.

The irritating events of the afternoon and
evening before slid into their correct place in the
rational light of a new day—the bickering
between herself and that mixed-up man were of
little consequence to her today. She scrubbed
her face with vigour, heart beating faster than
usual, longing to start her new job.

She dressed with care. Unfair though it might
seem, the clothes that a woman doctor wore
were important. In many hospitals jeans or
indeed any kind of trousers were *out*. It was a
rule which was unstated, but a rule none the
less which most of the women adhered to.
Anything too frivolous, too obviously feminine,
was frowned upon as well, so frills or very short
skirts would not find favour with the hierarchy.
The idea, she had decided long ago, was to
sublimate their sexuality in as attractive a way
as possible!

She donned a knee-length black skirt, teamed
with a dark green shirt of shot silk which she
had picked up in the sales. Matching dark green
woollen tights and slim black patent shoes gave
her a neat, co-ordinated appearance and she
tied her dark chestnut waves into a pony-tail at
the nape of her neck with a broad black velvet
ribbon.

That done, she pulled on her white coat and
checked the pockets for the equipment she

would need each day on the wards. Stetho-scope, patella hammer, ophthalmoscope and auroscope. She carried a book which listed all the commonly used drugs, their side-effects and contra-indications, and a thick black pocket notebook which she would shortly begin filling in with the names and diagnoses of all her new patients.

She was to report to Dale Ward at eight-thirty, where she would meet the rest of the team for a 'breakfast' meeting. Her new consultant was Dr Stanley Fenton-Taylor and she couldn't wait to meet him. She had been interested in cardiology since her pre-clinical days as a student, reading the erudite yet intriguing books on this specialist subject with fervour. When she had learned that she had gained a job on his firm, she had been disbelieving, then overjoyed, and it had made up for her decision to leave Barts. It had been a prize which had come at the end of the worst period of her life—and if it hadn't completely compensated for the events which had occurred, then it had certainly made her view her future with an entirely different attitude.

The flat *was* deserted, and she made herself some coffee which she drank down quickly and afterwards washed and dried the cup up. All was neat and tidy, so he must have washed up after their omelette last night. Well, she wouldn't have to tolerate such a touchy flatmate for much longer. And, by the end of her first day's work she would be able to come and pick up her belongings and move to somewhere more congenial.

It was a bleak, dull October morning with a fine grey drizzle in the air, and by the time she had walked over to the main building to Dale Ward a few wispy curls had escaped from the stark lines of her pony-tail, giving her face a sweetly feminine appearance.

She found the ward easily enough, and tapped on the door of Sister's office. She wanted to follow all the protocol of hospital life correctly; she knew from experience how first impressions counted and if she wanted to be liked by the ward staff, then she must make sure she was suitably polite and likeable.

'Sister' turned out to be surprisingly young—possibly even younger than Louisa herself, a tall girl with luminous green eyes smiling at her from behind dark-rimmed glasses. She stood up as Louisa entered the room and held out her hand.

'Hi,' she said. 'You must be our new house officer—I'm Amanda Patterson—known as Mandy—we don't stand on ceremony much here!'

Louisa shook the proffered hand. 'I'm pleased to hear it! Louisa Gray—nice to meet you.'

'The breakfast meeting has already started,' explained Mandy. 'I think they always tell you to come along a little later on your first day. It's held in the large interview room at the end of the ward. Come with me and I'll show you.'

'Thanks,' said Louisa, following her out of the office and on to the ward, trying to quash the feelings of nervousness which had suddenly arisen. She didn't really like the thought of trooping in late in front of the whole team.

'Has Dr Fenton-Taylor arrived yet?' she enquired.

Mandy turned to her in surprise. 'Oh, but he's in America until Christmas—didn't you know?'

Louisa digested this surprising piece of information. 'No, I didn't know.'

'But don't worry,' smiled Mandy. 'One of the Research Fellows is standing in for him.'

They walked down the highly polished floor of the aisle between the beds and she could see patients watching her curiously. As they passed one elderly woman's bed she heard her comment to her neighbour.

'Bit young for a doctor, ain't she?'

Louisa had to hide a smile and Mandy grinned at her conspiratorially.

'Don't worry, they'll soon get used to you. They keep telling me that *I'm* too young to be a sister—it's obviously not just policemen who start to look younger as one gets older!' They were both laughing as she pushed open a door and Louisa was confronted by the sight of about nine men in white coats, sitting around in easy chairs in a circle and drinking cups of coffee.

'Good luck,' whispered Mandy. 'Gentlemen—this is your new house officer!'

Louisa smiled nervously and looked around, trying to take it all in. As with all large groups of people, it took a moment for her mind to clear enough to look at them as individuals.

Some warning sound was clicking furiously in her mind, and her eyes travelled to the centre of the group, to the man who was obviously in charge of the proceedings. Now getting to his feet, moving his long legs reluctantly, watching her with an expression on his face which was not quite a smile—she found herself staring into the face of Adam Forrester.

'Dr Gray, I presume?' he asked and she nodded automatically, still too shocked by his appearance to say anything.

'I shall be standing in for Dr Fenton-Taylor until he returns from the States. Shall I introduce you to the rest of the team?' he was saying smoothly, guiding her by the arm until she stood in the centre, with all the uplifted, interested masculine faces greeting her. She hardly took a word in.

'Basil James is my registrar and Huw Lloyd is our SHO. The other reprobates you see before you are a handful of medical students, who I'm afraid will be astounding you with their appalling lack of knowledge over the next few weeks.' There were cries of dissent at this. 'Oh, and by the way—I'm Adam Forrester, Research Fellow.'

The turquoise eyes were hard and cold as they stared at her and her heart sank. Of all the unfair twists of fate. She had been rude and retaliatory to a man who was effectively going to be her boss for the next eight weeks or so. And while she didn't consider her response to his bad temper to be unjustified, she was far too intelligent to put her career on the line just in order to get her own back verbally. What on earth would he say to Dr Fenton-Taylor—the man on whom she would be relying for a reference? Damn, damn and damn!

Refusing a cup of coffee, she sat down to join in the meeting. She would just have to work like a Trojan. She imagined that the brittle Adam Forrester could be a hard taskmaster—she had better give him no opportunity to criticise her.

He had seated himself in a chair opposite her. 'We've almost finished discussing the patients— the main ward round isn't until tomorrow afternoon, so you've time before that to get to know some of the diagnoses. After we've finished here, I'll show you where our other ward is and you can meet the staff there.'

She nodded and listened while he began talking about a patient who was suffering from the rare condition of Takayasu's disease. One of the students hadn't heard of it and asked a question. She watched with interest as he changed the tack of his talk, switching from esoteric deliberation to a simple yet unpatronising explanation which the student appeared to grasp quite easily. It seemed that he knew his stuff.

The dark head had turned in her direction. 'Perhaps Dr Gray might be able to enlighten you on the aetiology of this syndrome?'

All the heads had swivelled in her direction— talk about being put on the spot! She began to rack her brain for the causes, when suddenly, to her relief, the facts came rushing back to her in the same smooth sequence that she'd learnt them from her textbook. Facts. Reliable, conclusive facts. Thank heavens for facts!

She recounted all that he had asked her fluently and at the end of her talk she saw that she had their total attention—she even thought she had noticed a rather grudging nod from Dr Forrester—but on that she could have been mistaken! At any rate, she had passed her first test with flying colours.

'Not bad,' he remarked, getting to his feet. 'I think that's all for today, everyone. Let's go over to Belling now, Dr Gray.'

She followed him up the ward, having to move quickly in an effort to emulate his long-legged stride. As he passed the ward office, Mandy came out with a drug chart for him to sign which he did willingly enough, even muttering an aside which produced a wide grin from the ward sister. Mandy, for one, seemed to find him pleasant enough, Louisa thought.

The lift doors slid open and they stepped inside. It was empty save for them, and she was immediately aware of the enforced silence and lack of eye contact which travelling in a lift always seemed to provoke, but she wanted to clear the air.

'Did you know that I was going to be working with you?' she asked, staring up at him.

He shrugged. 'I knew that I had a new house-man starting, yes, and I knew that it was a woman. Once I'd found out that you were a doctor, I didn't need the ability of Einstein to work out that you were most probably that person.'

She was furious. 'But you didn't think it prudent to tell me that you were my new boss?' she demanded.

'Slightly difficult, as you refused to tell me your name!'

He had conveniently forgotten that the reason for that was because he had embarrassed her so hatefully. 'This is going to make things very difficult, isn't it?'

He frowned. 'On the contrary—if you're moving out and our only contact is through work, then provided you do your job properly, I can anticipate no problems. I have no intention of letting a personality clash jeopardise your future—if that's what you're afraid of.'

It took the most monumental effort on her part not to snap back at him, but she forced herself to concentrate on why she was here—not to engage in a bickering match with some egocentric ex-media star, but to work!

She cleared her throat. 'Would you mind

telling me exactly how many medical beds we have?'

He clapped his hand to his forehead in an expression of mock amazement.

'Unbelievable! It only took you three minutes to get your mind back on to the job—not bad for a woman!'

She deserved it, she knew that—but it did not make the criticism any less easy to bear. She *had* been tittle-tattling like an overgrown school-girl and that, on top of everything else, would do little to improve his opinion of her. He probably had her firmly registered in his mind as a vacuous, immature female doctor who couldn't keep her mind on her job for more than a second. And she knew how much first impressions counted. . .

'I'm sorry,' she said stiffly. 'I'll make sure it doesn't happen again.'

The lift shuddered to a halt and he stood aside to let her pass.

'We have forty beds, divided into the two wards—twenty on Belling, which is male, and twenty on Dale, which is female. In addition we have a five-bedded coronary care unit attached to Belling—and Dr Fenton-Taylor guards these jealously.'

'What's he like?' she asked.

She saw a small frown cross his forehead while he considered the question.

'Like?' There was a pause. 'He's like most

consultants of his generation and ability—brilliant, autocratic, occasionally intolerant.'

A suprisingly honest appraisal, she decided as she walked up the wide corridor beside him, but he spoilt it all with his next comment.

'He likes good-looking women around,' he said, his lip curling in an expression of derision. 'So you should be all right.'

He was not going to get away with that.

'You'd better get this straight,' she stated forthrightly. 'I have *never* traded on being a woman to get on in life, and I don't intend to start now!'

He laughed. 'No? A woman who doesn't flutter her lashes and squeeze out every bit of sex appeal she's got? Surely a contradiction in terms, Dr Gray?'

How bitter he sounded. She turned flashing dark blue eyes on him.

'A medical version of the casting couch, you mean? Hardly, Dr Forrester—or else I might have been tempted to hang around the sitting-room late last night to take you up on your. . .er. . .offer.'

Their argument was abruptly terminated by their arrival at the ward, but she couldn't miss the look he gave her. It seemed that he was very good at dishing out nasty little comments, but not so good at taking them!

He marched on to Belling with her at his side, taking her straight into the office to meet Sister. The cold-eyed blonde who jumped to her feet to greet him could hardly have been more different from the cheery Mandy Patterson. Her sister's uniform of dark navy with white spots looked as though it were a size too small since it clung provocatively to her body in a way that no functional nurses' uniform was supposed to.

The ash-coloured hair was drawn back from her face and neck in the regulation manner, but small fair tendrils had been teased out, so that it looked more like the coiffure on a classical Greek statue than the working hairstyle of a busy ward sister. Large eyes of the palest grey were skilfully made even bigger by the expert use of sooty shadow and mascara.

Irreverently, Louisa was reminded of the old nursery tale 'Oh, Grandmama—what big eyes you have.' Now here, she thought, was someone who *did* use sex appeal almost as second nature. It would be interesting to see whether Adam Forrester objected to this kind of treatment.

The husky voice matched the body and the hair and the eyes perfectly.

'Adam!' she exclaimed warmly, the glossy lips glimmering into a perfect smile. 'I'll come round with you.'

It sounded as if she were conferring the highest honour in the land on him, Louisa thought with amusement, watching to see what the interaction was between them, surprised and slightly disappointed to see him return her treacly smile with an amicable grin.

'I've brought along my new house officer, Magda. I'd like you to meet Louisa Gray. Louisa—this is Sister Magda Maguire.'

She must have noticed Louisa standing at Adam's side, but the grey eyes turned towards her now for the first time, the smile dimming fractionally, the eyes frankly assessing. Or was she just being paranoid? Had Adam Forrester's unwelcoming behaviour made her expectations of St Dunstan's totally unrealistic—and was she misinterpreting a simple look?

But she knew that many nurses resented female doctors, resented their proximity and relationship with their male colleagues. Lots of nurses still behaved in a very territorial way towards doctors, and in years gone by women doctors had posed little threat—their numbers had been so small. But today, when they comprised almost half the intake of medical students. . .Well, Magda Maguire need have no concern on her account—she would rather spend a weekend with a man-eating tiger than spend an evening in the company of the foul-tempered Dr Forrester.

'Hello, there!' smiled Magda. 'Louisa, wasn't it? You must tell me all about yourself. Where did you do your training?'

'At Barts.' Louisa prayed that she didn't sound too much on the defensive.

'Really?' The other woman looked interested. 'I *am* impressed! One of London's most famous hospitals—and yet you decided not to do any of your house jobs there?'

The inevitable question. 'No. I wanted to come to St Dunstan's.'

'Oh?' Magda seemed to be expecting more, but she could whistle for it, thought Louisa stubbornly, knowing all the time how weak and feeble her explanation sounded. Because, although St Dunstan's was a well-respected and busy general hospital, it carried none of the élitism and status attached to St Bartholomew's—known to its staff as 'God's own hospital'.

The grey eyes stared at her reproachfully for a moment, then turned to gaze fondly on Adam.

'Would you like me to show her the ward? Leave you to have your coffee and do your paperwork in peace?'

He looked at Louisa for a moment, then nodded his agreement.

'That would be a great help. Is that all right with you, Dr Gray?'

How formal he was with her! 'Perfectly. Thanks, Sister.' She was aware that her voice sounded stiff, starchy even.

She left the office, following the neat, swinging rear of Magda Maguire, feeling disgruntled. The day had got off to a bad start, and there was no doubt in her mind who was responsible.

CHAPTER FOUR

IT WAS her first full day as a working doctor and she was mentally and physically unprepared for the sheer hard work, the relentless pace of it, and the demands. As a student she had done a 'shadow'—tailing the house officer for four weeks, to give her a taste of the job. But this time she was on her own. True, she had her SHO, her registrar, and ultimately her consultant to call upon, but she had been taught as a medical student not to abuse the back-up system. They each had a heavy work-load—she must get on as best she could, save in a real emergency where she felt unable to cope.

Magda Maguire had pointed out the geography of the ward, and then taken her to each patient, where Louisa had quickly written down their name and initial diagnosis, intending to bone up on them that evening so that she was fairly well acquainted with them in time for tomorrow's ward round.

Then she returned to Dale and did the same there, and Mandy Patterson made her a cup of coffee for which Louisa was extremely grateful, but she had no chance to drink more than a couple of mouthfuls, and by the time she

returned it had formed a thick skin and had to
be thrown away.

And in between trying to learn all about forty
new patients and their illnesses, she was having
to deal with some of the problems which had
arisen overnight, and non-urgent problems
from the preceding weekend. One patient had
developed a livid red rash after being com-
menced on a new drug treatment. Another's
intravenous infusion had 'tissued'—the cannula
had slipped out of the vein into the surrounding
tissue—and it took Louisa ages to resite, partly
because she was not yet very practised at it, but
the sound of Magda Maguire clicking her tongue
impatiently beside her did little to improve her
confidence.

Lunch consisted of a hastily eaten cheese and
tomato sandwich which she had in the canteen
with Huw the houseman, and Basil the registrar. Huw was a swarthy Welshman with jet
black hair and dark eyes. They chatted mainly
about the patients, and were just swallowing
down the last of their drinks when he turned to
her.

'I wanted to ask you a favour,' he smiled,
showing a lot of very white teeth. 'I'm booked
in to play a game of squash at six, but we've a
GP admission arriving later this afternoon. Be
an angel, would you Louisa, and clerk him in
for me? You're on call tonight anyway, aren't
you?'

'Sounds OK to me,' she agreed. 'What's the matter with him?'

Huw scowled. 'God knows why he's being admitted—the father is a friend of Fenton-Taylor, apparently. He's a young guy of twenty-three who's been presenting with attacks of breathlessness and palpitations, but you've only to know the rest of his family to suspect that all he's suffering from is nerves.'

Louisa personally detested this kind of judge-mental diagnosis, but she said nothing, merely smiled at Huw and said she'd see him later.

'Just do a history, and then we'll sit on him tonight—don't bother ordering any tests until Adam's seen him on the ward round,' were his parting words.

She spent the rest of the afternoon to and fro between Dale and Belling. Adam was holding an Outpatients' Clinic and so Basil dealt with medical emergencies through the Casualty Department. That day, and for the night to come, their team was on 'take', which meant that any patient turning up at the Accident and Emergency Department with a medical problem which required admission would automatically be admitted by Dr Fenton-Taylor's team.

Just after five o'clock, Huw's patient was admitted to Belling and, after he had been undressed and had his observations done by the nurse, Louisa took a set of notes along to his bed.

She was slightly bemused when she saw him

and couldn't quite work out why. He had thick wavy hair which cascaded to his shoulders, almost in the manner of a fifteenth-century nobleman! Instead of conventional pyjamas, he was wearing a top and trousers which looked very definitely Eastern—birds and butterflies embroidered brightly on the back and on the collar. And he had a curiously angular, interesting face, the kind of face you would not forget in a hurry. She suddenly realised why he was not what she had expected—when Huw had told her that the patient was known by the consultant, she had automatically assumed that she would be examining a very normal, proper young English gentleman—not the exotic creature who sat grinning at her.

'You're admiring my hair, Doctor?' he laughed.

'It's unusual,' she admitted, pulling up a chair beside the bed and sitting down.

'Very necessary for my work. I paint,' he explained.

'The appearance of the artist hasn't altered much over hundreds of years, has it?' She smiled, putting two fingers lightly on the brachial pulse in his wrist.

She asked him all about his attacks, writing down their onset, frequency and duration. She asked him all about his childhood illnesses, his way of life, his diet and whether he smoked or drank. Then she examined him thoroughly, listening to his heart and lungs, palpating his abdomen, and testing all his reflexes. The standard history-taking which all patients underwent.

After she had completed everything, she remembered Huw telling her not to bother with tests until he had been seen on the ward round, but something was niggling away at her. Late onset attacks—discovered usually in early childhood. She felt that she knew the answer, but that it was eluding her. Could the attacks be an allergy to any of the materials he used in his work as an artist? She quizzed him thoroughly, but came to a dead end.

Then something else occurred to her. 'Have you ever had an ECG?' she asked him.

He grimaced. 'Sounds painful.'

She shook her head. 'Well, it isn't. Its proper name is an electrocardiogram. We attach some leads to your chest, and connect them to a machine so that we can see what your heart is doing. The machine traces out a kind of graph which can give us a lot of information. I think I'm going to get one done on you this evening.'

She glanced at her watch—it was just gone six. She wondered whether the ECG technician had already gone home. She went in search of the staff nurse who had replaced Magda at the end of her shift.

'No, you won't get a technician now,' she told her. 'They knock off at five-thirty sharp. Not like doctors and nurses!'

'Damn,' said Louisa softly. It *could* wait until

morning, but she had wanted time to study the tracing properly.

'Tell you what,' said the other girl helpfully. 'We've got our own ECG in coronary care—it's not quite so sophisticated as the other one, but it's good enough. Do you know how to use it?'

Louisa shook her head—today she had realised that she might now be a qualified doctor, but that there were a great many things she didn't know!

'Well, I can. Things are quiet now before supper—come with me and I'll show you.'

Half an hour later, Louisa had her ECG, and was fully *au fait* with how to use the machine. She had planned to go to supper when her bleep began shrieking in the pocket of her white coat.

She went to the phone in the office. 'Dr Gray,' she said to the telephonist. 'Someone's bleeping me.'

'Just a moment, please,' intoned the sing-song voice at the other end. There was a click and a pause, and then a deep voice which she recognised instantly.

'Dr Gray?' it barked impatiently. 'Where the hell are you?'

'I've been clerking a patient for Huw,' she replied, looking at herself in the age-spotted mirror opposite, and wishing that her hair didn't resemble something that you might find in a bowl of Chinese soup.

'God, he's a lazy so-and-so.' She could hear

Adam muttering. 'You realise we're on call together? I've got an admission coming in through Casualty, so you'd better come over.'

She had *not* realised that she was on call with him—although if she'd thought about it long enough she would have done. After all, he had been off at the weekend too. For a moment she almost laughed at the irony of it—fate seemed to be conspiring to push together two people who couldn't stand the sight of each other! Working together, on call together, living together. Living together! With a horrified jolt she remembered that she had done nothing about changing her accommodation—she'd scarcely had a chance to draw breath all day, let alone go and see the administrator. Well, it was too bad, it would just have to wait until tomorrow now.

She made her way to Casualty easily enough, and found him in the office, studying an X-ray. The first thing that came to mind when she saw him was how unfair the gods were in distributing their gifts to mankind. She had often thought that the white coat of a doctor—synonymous as it was with power and intelligence—could transform even the most weedy little man. And when someone with all the physical attributes of Adam Forrester was wearing it, well, even she had to admit that it made him almost indecently good-looking.

He turned around and the turquoise eyes bored into her, a puzzled expression on his face.

'What is it?' he asked.

She must have been standing and staring at him like a gormless idiot! And what could she say? Sorry, didn't mean to subject you to an intense scrutiny, but I was just thinking what an attractive picture you made! She said the first thing that came into her head.

'I haven't had a chance to speak to the administrator all day—I'm sorry. So I'm afraid I'm in the flat for one more night, but I'll definitely go and see her tomorrow.'

To her surprise he didn't immediately bite her head off.

'Yes, yes. Don't worry about it. Tomorrow will do.' He turned back to his X-ray. 'I'm expecting an admission—an overdose. Come and look at this while we're waiting. It's a patient I've got in one of the cubicles, he came to my Outpatients' Clinic.'

She stood before the chest X-ray, unable to see any abnormality at all, until he pointed out the notching of the ribs, due to coarctation of the aorta.

When he spoke about it, he spoke passionately, with the fervour and enthusiasm of the true scientist. He made it sound so easy! She wondered what he would be like dealing with patients—often the most brilliant minds who became doctors were hopeless at interacting well with the people they were treating. Often, she suspected, because most medical practitioners came from the middle classes and went

straight from school to medical school, gaining
little experience of life on the way. It sometimes
took many years before they learned how to deal
with people, and some never learned the knack.

'You'd better check the blood pressure in both
arms,' he told her. 'There's bound to be a
difference in pressure on both sides, depending
which side the coarctation is on.'

She did as he asked and returned with the
two different readings for him.

'You've worked in Casualty before, I take it?'

She nodded. 'Just as a receptionist in the long
vacation, a couple of years ago—not as a
student, so I won't know much.'

'That's better than nothing. Don't tell me—
you were a hard-up student, saving for a holiday in the sun?'

It was a pity that his first attempt at polite
conversation should have embraced a subject
which she most definitely did not want to
pursue. She looked away hastily, her heart
thudding, remembering the reasons which had
necessitated her taking the holiday job, and
terrified that he would begin to pry if he saw
the expression on her face.

'I see you have a red phone here,' she said
hurriedly. 'Is that for emergencies only?'

If he had noticed her sudden change of subject, he made no comment, merely nodded.
'Yes. That's a direct line from ambulance control. I'll ask Sister to get them to ring the number
for you later, it has quite a different tone—much

shriller and harsher. You're expected to answer it if you're here on your own.'

They heard the distant wail of an ambulance siren, growing closer all the time. The screech of brakes. The slam of doors.

'Sounds like our case,' he said gruffly.

It was. The ambulancemen carried in the semi-conscious form of a young woman who looked to be in her late twenties, and Louisa was shocked by the grey pallor of her skin. She was dressed in a thin sweater and ill-fitting skirt, with no stockings—entirely inappropriate garb for the cold October evening. On her cheek was the livid saffron and magenta of a fading bruise. Louisa thought that she had never seen anyone look so pitiful in her whole life.

As they lifted her from the stretcher to the trolley, a crumpled photograph fluttered from the woman's handbag and as Louisa bent to retrieve it, it caught her eye. It was the angelic face of a blond-haired toddler, his fringe cut at an odd angle as he smiled warily at the camera. On the bottom of the photograph was scrawled 'Bobby'.

She replaced it sadly in the handbag, wondering who was looking after that small boy at the moment.

A staff nurse appeared and directed the trolley to one of the larger cubicles. Meanwhile Adam stood talking intently to the distraught-looking older woman who had accompanied the patient. He came over to Louisa a few moments later.

'That's the girl's mother,' he explained. 'She thinks she must have taken the tablets just over an hour ago. That's quite good from our point of view—not too much will have been absorbed. She's taken Triptisol, which she was receiving from her GP for depression—her mother quite wisely brought the bottle in. She thinks that it probably contained about fifteen tablets, so we'll do a stomach wash-out straight away.'

The next half-hour passed in a frenzy of activity—Louisa watching while the nurses donned huge plastic aprons before inserting a large rubber tube down the girl's throat into her stomach, then adding water and forcing her to vomit. Louisa wondered what had caused this young woman to take the desperate measure of trying to end her own life. She watched as she retched into a bucket, her arms flailing as she tried to pull the tube out.

Adam seemed satisified with the result. 'But I'm sending her up to ITU—we're almost empty there at the moment, and she can be watched overnight. Because, as I expect you know, there can be dangerous side-effects even from a fairly small non-fatal overdose.'

'Cardiac arrhythmias?' queried Louisa.

He nodded. 'Exactly. I'd like you to put a drip up on her before she goes up. In the morning, when she's woken up a bit, you can take a full history. She might need a psychiatric referral—she'll almost certainly need some counselling, and to be seen by a social worker.'

'It's terrible to see someone of your own age lying there,' Louisa blurted out. 'To think that her life was such a black hole that she could see no way out other than death.'

He shook his head very slightly. 'Let me give you a tip. If you feel like getting involved, then *don't*. If you want to be a good doctor you just can't afford to. Unless you can give the patient impartial, not impassioned advice, you won't be doing them, or yourself, any good. It's a hard enough job, both mentally and physically, without adding to it by taking unnecessary emotions on board.'

She nodded. 'Point taken. I'll try to remember.'

He glanced at his watch. 'Have you been round the wards?'

'About an hour ago. No problems then—I re-sited Mr Wightwick's IVI, and it's running through nicely now.'

'Good. When you've finished here you might as well go and get some supper and some rest. If it's a busy take we could be up all night.'

He turned abruptly on his heel and left the department and she was left staring after him. What a strange man he was, she thought as she watched the nurse lay up a trolley for her. As a doctor, she couldn't fault him. Already she felt as though she had learnt heaps today. Instinc-tively, she knew that Adam Forrester was going to prove a fine teacher.

But his grumpy arrogance towards her in his

flat had shown that he could be a real Jekyll and Hyde, and she smiled at the comparison between the two doctors. Perhaps he was simply the solitary type, who didn't like anyone intruding on his space.

Still, if tomorrow she found herself a different flat, and if he continued to be as helpful and as instructive as he had been today, then her time at St Dunstan's was going to prove very useful indeed.

There was a new lightness about her step as she headed off towards the canteen. She even managed to eat her fish and salad without being bleeped, so she decided to make the most of her spare time and go back to the flat and study Justin's ECG.

She let herself in quietly, but it was dark and she heaved a sigh of relief when she realised that it was empty. Dr Forrester was a lot more formidable on his home ground than he was in his lofty position of temporary consultant!

She spread the ECG out on her desk. She was now almost sure of her diagnosis, but she got one of her textbooks out anyway, her finger running swiftly down paragraph after paragraph as she gathered together all the information she was seeking.

And she had it! It was all there—early adult onset, attacks of breathlessness and palpitations—and the classic ECG with its reduced PR interval in the delta wave confirmed it. Justin de Havilland was suffering from the electro-physiological condition of the heart known as Wolff-Parkinson-White's syndrome.

He was not 'neurotic', and his presenting signs were not masking a more sinister under-lying condition. He could be treated effectively by anti-arrhythmic drugs.

Eureka! She felt an enormous rush of pleasure and remembered that *this* was why she had studied so hard to become a doctor.

She wrote copious notes on the condition, her hand aching as she did so, scarcely aware that her eyelids were growing heavier and heavier. . .

She came to as if her senses had been drugged, dragging herself towards the voice which called her name. She felt hands, strong hands on her shoulders, felt warm breath near her face. And suddenly it all came rushing back—the longing, the loneliness and the desperation. Nights spent awake, teeth gritted, knuckles clenched, tossing and turning amid the rumpled sheets—wonder-ing what she should have done differently—not to have driven him away.

But now the spell had been broken. He had come back. She could smell the seductive mas-culine scent of him. Her hands went up to lock firmly at the back of his neck, and she clung to him furiously, strength and comfort emanating from the firm muscles of his chest. He had come back!

And then her arms were being firmly disentangled and a moan of objection escaped from her lips. Through the dizzying mists of her dream she heard the voice saying her name again. But she felt a vague quiver of alarm as she realised with a shock that it was not Mike's voice that called her.

Her eyes snapped open and she looked aghast into eyes of turquoise-blue—his face so close to hers that if she had bent her head forward just a fraction, then her hair would have tumbled all over him. She could feel his warm breath on her lips and for one crazy moment she thought that he was about to kiss her. A loud pulse began singing and racing and roaring in her ears.

The turquoise eyes narrowed consideringly, as though he were searching the very depths of her mind.

'Wh—what happened?' she croaked, through dry lips.

'Happened?' He gave a short laugh. 'You were dead to the world, not answering your bleep. I came in to find you asleep over your textbooks, and when I tried to rouse you—you appeared to be having some kind of nightmare.' He smiled. 'I can only think that last night's cheese omelette must have been responsible!'

His joke managed to relieve some of the tension, and she was grateful to him. Thank heaven he had been diplomatic enough to stop things when he had or what else might have happened?

He moved towards the door. 'We've got an old chap with emphysema coming in—I'll wait outside for you, if you want to wake up properly.'

'Thanks.'

She picked up her hairbrush and gazed at herself in the mirror, noting her flushed cheeks and dilated pupils. It was clear the message that her body was sending out, she thought.

That there were a lot worse places you could wake up than in Adam Forrester's arms.

CHAPTER FIVE

THEY didn't get back until three a.m. After admitting the wheezy, chesty old man with emphysema, there was a small spate of emergencies during which both of them worked flat out.

He said not one word about her 'nightmare' and, when she thought of the mileage he could have made of it, she decided that the Jekyll in him must be dominant this evening! Perhaps she should have tried to explain—but how would the truth have sounded? 'Sorry—but I thought you were my ex-husband.'

When they arrived back at the flat, Adam said goodnight and went straight to his room.

Louisa brushed her teeth and washed at speed, and crept thankfully into bed. But the sleep which she sought, and which her body so needed, did nothing but evade her. Her limbs felt heavy and exhausted, but it was her mind which stubbornly refused to give her peace, chasing the same thoughts round and around inside her head. Thoughts of Mike. Thoughts which she would rather have go away. She hadn't permitted herself any thoughts of Mike for a long time now. That had been part of her own prescription for recovery.

* * *

She had been just nineteen when they had married, against everyone's advice. It was easy to see now, of course, just why the wedding had been so opposed. It had been more than their youth, and their immaturity—it was their basic incompatibility. But with the fierce determination of their years they had resisted all attempts to part them.

She realised now that, left completely alone by college tutors, deans, parents and her aunt, the relationship would most probably have fizzled out on its own.

Part of the problem had been her own sheltered upbringing. After the death of her parents in an automobile accident, she had been sent to a remote part of Cornwall to be brought up by Beatrice, her mother's sister, and her only living relative.

She had been a naturally bright student, and her aunt had pushed her to succeed. On evenings when her peers were giggling their way to the cinema or to one of the small cafés down near the harbour, she sat poring over her science books. And when she won the coveted scholarship to St Bartholomew's, everyone had told her how lucky she was, how she mustn't let them down. She had felt that she had a lot to live up to.

So that when she arrived at the vast London medical school, she was academically superior to almost all her year, but emotionally still a child. She had learned very quickly how to make the others laugh, that she could be as witty as they were. She learned too that to hide the glorious waves of her dark red hair in the constricting bun which her aunt had always insisted on did her no justice at all.

And gradually, with the soft unpinned hair, came make-up—not a great deal of it, just enough to enhance the intriguing almond shape of her sapphire eyes, and the pale skin and the full lips. Naturally she noticed the second glances which she began attracting, but had paid little heed to them because through all her physical metamorphosis she remained passionately commited to and spellbound by medical science. She enjoyed casual drinks with the crowd and saw the occasional film, or sat in the gods at the Royal Albert Hall, listening to music by the great composers, but, for the most part, she continued to spend much of her spare time studying. None of the male medical students had interested her in the least.

Until Mike had come along, and sought an introduction into her circle. A fourth-year student, he had been flavour of the year with his blond and dashing good looks, and his talents as actor, sportsman and raconteur. He had a reputation for loving attractive women, which he lived up to. Louisa knew *of* him, naturally. But the breezy college hero held no lure for her.

Perhaps that was what did it. Her smiling lack of interest had seemed to inflame him, like a moth to a candle. She found that wherever she went, he seemed to be there too. In the library he insisted on sharing a table with her. He carried her books to the canteen for her. He was in love.

Few women could have resisted his attentions for as long as Louisa did, and very cautiously she began to care for him, too. She was attracted to him, but she was afraid, unsure whether she could cope with a love affair at this stage in her life. She tried hard to quash the belief that to go to bed with him was wrong. It wasn't, it was perfectly natural. Everyone else was doing it.

Still she hesitated, and her hesitation and her purity inflamed him even more—her elusiveness had become integral to the relationship. He *had* to have her. More than that—theirs was to be the greatest of student love affairs—they would get married.

It was a small register office wedding, and afterwards there was a huge party in the students' common room, where, egged on by his friends, Mike drank a yard of ale and was violently sick. And so began their married life together.

It was terrifying how quickly the gilt faded. They soon found that two people could not live as cheaply as one, and that a room meant for one person could soon become too small when two people were arguing in it.

The arguments started when each realised that the other had no intention of changing. After the honeymoon period, Louisa fully expected them both to study companionably together in the evenings. Mike did not. He wanted them to continue with the cinema and the bar, spending their already frugal grants on having a good time. And anyway, he had told her with a grin, he had spent his whole life breezing through exams.

But it was alien to Louisa's character to turn her back on the hard work she knew was necessary to get her the good grades she craved for. At first she tried compromising, going out with him when he wanted her to, until his complaints about her grudging company became hard to take.

'It's a peculiar type of girl who favours a textbook rather than her husband,' he had sneered once.

In the end she had returned to spending her evenings studying, and Mike would come in just before midnight, blurry-eyed, just as she was packing her books up.

At weekends she did not work, and turned eagerly to him, but he seemed filled with a new kind of restlessness, which he refused to discuss.

And the physical side of their marriage she instinctively felt had disappointed him. Soon, bitter recriminations began to be hurled at her— that she had bartered her body for marriage— and what a poor deal he had made. She had known how experienced he had been, but he made her feel stupid for her lack of it. Love-making seemed to be a hurried demonstration of his prowess, rather than the magical act of union she had imagined.

She had become increasingly consumed by guilt, aware that she had been gathered up and swept away by the romantic momentum of his courtship of her, and had agreed to marry him in an emotional state of adolescent turmoil.

The relationship was in a downward spiral, and then came Mike's finals. She had bullied him to work, which he did, but never, she feared, quite enough. When the results were pinned up on to the noticeboard, her worst fears had been confirmed. Mike had not just 'breezed through' this one. No, indeed. He was one of only three people in the year who had failed.

She had not been able to find him anywhere. She had looked in the bar, the squash courts, asked his friends. No one seemed to know, but one or two had eyed her shiftily, she thought.

She'd unlocked the door to their tiny flat to find the pale, chubby limbs of a student nurse wrapped around his naked body. He had glanced up from his exploration of the girl's neck, and when she had looked into his flushed, disorientated face—she'd felt that she was look-ing into the face of a stranger.

To Louisa, it had seemed a stage-managed, humiliating betrayal. She had moved out shortly afterwards, to discover that he had not only cleared out all the funds in their joint account, but had left it badly overdrawn. His parents, he had informed her glibly, would pay his half; she would have to find her own.

This final act, following his infidelity, had almost broken her. She had cancelled the proposed long vacation with Aunt Beatrice to quietly lick her wounds. Instead she had taken the clerk's job in Casualty and had repaid the debt.

Six months later he had re-sat the exams and passed, and mercifully had done his house jobs elsewhere. Before he had left, they had agreed to a legal separation. But she had felt that she could never truly leave the bitter memories of the past behind her, until she had left St Bartholomew's itself. . .

Stretching long, slim legs, Louisa turned on to her side, reading the face on the small luminous travel clock which lay on her locker. Four-fifty. Hardly worth going to sleep really.

She got up and went over to the window, pulling aside the worn fabric of the curtain, but there was no sign of the dawn. A damp, dreary, drizzly morning. She'd had no sleep and had been lying awake for hours dissecting the ruins of her marriage. She should by rights have felt awful, but strangely enough she didn't. She felt more alive than she had done in ages, because she realised at last that she was free. For the first time in her whole life she was her own agent, to go in whatever direction she chose, and Mike was free as well. Glad, no doubt, to be without the burden of a wife to whom he could never really relate.

Tonight had been the first time that she had ever tried to pinpoint the failure in her marriage, and she had discovered that the fault had been hers too, not just Mike's.

She stretched, debating whether or not to lie down again, when the high-pitched tone of her bleep sounded. It was Sister in the Coronary Care Unit.

'Dr Gray? It's about Mr Sanderson, our thirty-eight-year-old myocardial infarction patient who's now two days post-infarction.' Her voice sounded worried. 'He's been showing arrhythmias for about half an hour now and they're getting more frequent.'

'I'll be over right away,' said Louisa quickly.

'Do you want me to bleep Dr Forrester as well?'

Louisa paused for a moment. She was new, and she was inexperienced. She must never be afraid to ask for his expertise and guidance. It was the patient who counted.

'I think so. Yes, please.'

It occurred to her that she could have just walked across the hall and rapped on his door, but quickly rejected that idea as inappropriate.

She slipped her shoes and her white coat back on, brushed her hair and let herself out of the flat, hearing his bleep begin to shrill as she did so. She walked briskly over to CCU, her mind racing. A patient who had already had a severe heart attack was always potentially at risk from another, particularly in the early stages following the first attack.

She heard the faint sounds of machines as she walked into Mr Sanderson's cubicle, and saw the bright green tracing as it flickered across the monitor.

Not wanting to alarm the still drowsy patient any more than she needed to, she smiled briefly and said hello, before turning back towards the monitor, not liking what she saw there. The ventricular ectopics were now rushing across the screen. They were going to have to act quickly. Oh, please hurry, Adam, she prayed silently.

Her prayer was answered as he strode into the cubicle and stood next to the patient. He placed his fingers lightly on the pulse, watching the corresponding pattern on the ECG as he did so. He nodded and spoke quietly to Sister.

Sister nodded and reappeared seconds later with a kidney dish containing syringe and drug. Feeling slightly redundant, Louisa watched as the practised hands of the nurse swiftly snapped the top off the phial and drew it up into the syringe. Adam began to inject it slowly into the giving set of the infusion, and all three of them watched the monitor anxiously.

For a moment the erratic upward sweeps of the ventricular ectopics seemed to tail off, so that the reading became almost normal, when suddenly they began again without warning, and with renewed vigour.

'Ventricular tachycardia,' said Adam in a quiet voice. 'I think he might go into VF. Better get the paddles ready, Gwen.'

Louisa looked at him. She knew what he meant—he was about to give the patient an electric shock to get the heart back into normal rhythm, because ventricular tachycardia, when the electrical activity of the heart goes completely haywire, could lead to death.

She saw Gwen squirting great blobs of jelly on to the paddles of the large defibrillator in the corner, just as she heard a change in the tone of the monitor and the tracing begin to show crazy peaks on the screen.

'VF!' Adam's voice sounded almost resigned and she helped him pull back the thin white cotton gown to expose the patient's chest, as Gwen handed him the paddles. He placed one on each side of the sternum.

'Give me two hundred and fifty joules,' he commanded. 'And stand back!'

The button was pressed and the man's body twitched in a swift spasm as the power raced through his body. They waited breathlessly, but the monitor resumed its wild tracing.

'Let's try three hundred. Stand back!'

But the increased power still had no effect. The room was absolutely silent now, save for the ticking of the clock on the wall. Louisa noticed the paleness of the man's skin, and the

jelly which was now smeared over his chest.
She saw the sweat on Adam's brow.

'Three-fifty.' He held the paddles in place.
'Stand back!'

Nothing. No change. In a few moments it
would all be too late.

'Four hundred.'

She had never heard a voice sound so emo-
tionless. A few hours ago, this patient had been
sitting up in bed, talking and joking with his
wife and child, thinking himself over the worst
of his illness.

And now? If Adam Forrester and his four
hundred joules had no effect, then he would
simply no longer be a part of this world. Was
this what he had meant when he had told her
about not getting involved with patients? How
could you do your job properly if your heart
broke every time someone you had grown fond
of died? She closed her eyes and uttered a short,
fervent prayer.

'Stand back!' The familiar command made her
open them again. She saw the body almost
thrown a few inches off the bed as the electrical
current swept through Mr Sanderson. The
monitor seemed to freeze for a moment, and
then they all saw the most incredible thing. The
erratic tracing was no more and they saw a
smooth sinus rhythm tentatively streak across,
and again, and again. She heard a small sigh
escape from Adam's lips.

He smiled at them both. 'Thanks, Gwen. Thanks, Louisa.'

It was the first time he had called her directly by her Christian name, and she hadn't really done anything for him to thank her for, but she was too busy marvelling at the miracle of science she had just witnessed to care about anything else.

The three of them stood grinning foolishly at one another, a unit—the rest of the world excluded. It was a moment she would treasure long after other memories had faded from her mind.

'But he's not out of the woods yet, though,' Adam warned, glancing down at Louisa. 'We'll have to keep a close watch on him and keep our fingers crossed that he'll retain a steady sinus rhythm.'

He caught sight of the clock on the wall. It was now almost six-thirty and work on the wards began at eight. There would be no sleep for them now.

Gwen began bustling around Mr Sanderson, wiping dollops of conducting jelly away from his skin, and Louisa and Adam stood side by side, just listening to the comfortingly regular bleep of the monitor.

He almost smiled again. 'Thrown in at the deep end, weren't you? What did you think of your first night on call?'

She hesitated, her mind going over all that

had happened. Had it really only been twenty-four hours? But she'd learnt a lot, no question about it.

'Interesting,' she replied slowly. 'And instructive. Thank you.' She bent down to look at the drug chart, not wanting him to see the sudden rise in colour as she remembered clinging to him just hours earlier. She almost felt like adding 'highly disturbing' to her brief evaluation.

Through the large sheet glass window, she saw the first yellow and pink tinges of day streak the sky and then, incredibly, her bleep began to shrill once more.

It had been a long night.

CHAPTER SIX

IT WAS to prove an even longer day. Louisa had
to rush round all the patients, checking blood
results and X-rays for abnormalities and making
sure that these were all filed with the notes for
the grand ward round. From eight o'clock she
was no longer on call, so that at least her bleep
wasn't summoning her to Casualty for emergency admissions.

It was coffee-time before she managed to grab
a break, and sit and discuss her findings on
Justin de Havilland with Huw Lloyd. She'd had
no breakfast, and hardly paused for breath as
she hungrily munched a danish pastry washed
down with a cup of coffee.

'Busy?' enquired Huw, and she nodded
vigorously.

She replaced her cup on the saucer with a
sigh of satisfaction and pulled the ECG she had
done the evening before from her pocket,
spreading it on to the top of the stained formica
table in front of them.

'Listen,' she said without preamble. 'I don't
think that this chap is neurotic, and I think that
his palpitations and attacks of breathlessness
have a much surer foundation than hysteria.
Look at this ECG.'

73

She saw the Welshman's eyes narrow.

'I thought I told you not to bother ordering an ECG until after Adam had seen him?'

She turned to him in surprise. 'I know you did, but it suddenly occurred to me that I might know his diagnosis, which was only confirmable on an ECG. And anyway,' she added, mildly irritated by his pedantry, 'I didn't actually *order* one. I had a bit of free time and so I did it myself. As you had gone off to play squash, I could hardly bleep you to ask for your permission.' She knew she sounded sarcastic and grumpy, but frankly she couldn't care less. She was tired and she felt unappreciated. And Huw Lloyd was only the senior house officer, for goodness' sake. She couldn't imagine Adam ever pulling rank on her if he felt she had some valid point to make.

The handsome swarthy face peered down at the graph paper, his bottom lip sticking out like a small child's. 'All right then, cardiologist of the century. What did you find?'

She felt astonished. Surely he could see for himself? Surely he could see the dramatically reduced PR interval in the delta wave as clearly as daylight? A nagging voice in her head wondered whether he had actually heard of this particular cardiac disorder, and if he hadn't, then why on earth didn't he just ask her? His masculine ego, most probably, she surmised and if she hadn't felt so bone weary she might mischievously have tried to catch him out.

'I'm certain that he's got Wolff-Parkinson-White's,' she said, flicking back a thick lock of hair which had tumbled over the collar of her white coat. 'He's displayed all the signs— together with an early adult onset. This ECG shows a classic tracing.'

He picked it up and peered at it again. 'Er— yes, of course. I think you're right.' He popped it into his pocket. 'I'll have a good look at it myself, just to check that there aren't any other abnormal signs.'

He stood up to leave and she opened her mouth to protest, when she noticed that he wasn't even looking at her, but his eyes were following the retreating derriere of a tall, and exceedingly young student nurse. Again she felt irritated, but she didn't really have any grounds for refusing to let him borrow the ECG, did she? As she brushed the crumbs off her napkin, she reflected that there was something about Huw Lloyd that she didn't entirely like.

Before the grand round, she managed to get an appointment to see Mrs Jefferson, the administrator. She was ushered into her office by an elderly secretary and was slightly taken aback by the glamorous creature who sat behind the large polished mahogany desk, head bent, and writing furiously.

She looked up and smiled. 'Please sit down, Dr Gray,' she said in a low, pleasant voice. 'I'll be with you in one moment.'

Louisa sat down, welcoming a few moments

of peaceful uninterrupted rest, and began in a leisurely manner to survey her surroundings and their occupant.

The cut-glass vase of vast bronze chrysanthemum globes and the subtle splashily painted watercolour on the wall owed nothing to standard hospital issue. At one side of the desk stood a silver-framed photo of a fair-haired man laughing down into the face of a small girl who was a replica of himself. For a moment, Louisa felt a wave of something which almost felt like envy. The cool Mrs Jefferson seemed to have it all worked out—a job and a marriage which looked happy. It was every career woman's dream, and one which she somehow doubted ever achieving herself.

She looked more closely at the figure busy scribbling in the well-cut navy suit. She was about as far removed from the popular image of a fusty old hospital administrator as it was possible to get.

She laid her pen down and looked up at Louisa at last, smiling pleasantly, her dark hair falling in two silky wings to frame her face, the intelligent eyes curious. She pressed a small button on her desk and the grey-haired secretary bustled in to remove the batch of papers. They waited in silence until she had gone.

'Please forgive me, Dr Gray. I'm afraid that couldn't wait. Now——' she leaned back in her chair '—what exactly can I do for you—or can I guess? Does it concern Dr Forrester?'

Louisa nodded. 'Yes, indeed it does. I'd like to change flats, if that would be possible? I don't think that Dr Forrester is prepared to share his flat with a woman doctor, and to be honest—I'd prefer segregated accommodation myself.'

There was a mixture of amusement and concern on the administrator's face. 'I'm very sorry, but I'm going to have to say no. Even if I could make an exception, and to be perfectly frank— I'm just a little tired of Dr Forrester always insisting that exceptions be made for him—I'm afraid that I simply don't have another flat to offer you.

'The Nurses' Home is being renovated just now, so there's nowhere over there, and the rest of the medical block is fully occupied. Because of the price of rented accommodation in the town, I'm obliged to provide rooms for many of the paramedical staff here.'

She softened slightly at the sight of Louisa's expression of woe. 'I know he can be difficult, Dr Gray. The man is either an angel or a devil depending on where you view him from—as I know to my cost! He regards administrators as the petty cogs in a bureaucracy who will put every obstacle in his way to stop him saving lives! But it is only for six months, not a lifetime. Unless, of course——' she paused delicately '—there's a specific problem?'

Louisa wondered how the serene Mrs Jefferson would react if she informed her that she was slightly perturbed by her own reaction to Dr Forrester.

'There's no specific problem,' she lied. 'I dare say I can adapt. But if any other room should become vacant in the meantime. . .?'

'You'll be top of the list,' smiled the administrator, standing up to shake hands.

So that, thought Louisa as she hurried over to Belling Ward, was that. Barring a miracle, she was stuck with Adam Forrester, and he with her. And if he didn't like it, then let him go and see Mrs Jefferson to see if he could fare any better.

The moment she arrived back on the ward there was no time left to even think about her domestic arrangements. She and Magda Maguire had to pump a withdrawing alcoholic patient full of sedation and then move him to a side-ward where he would cause less disturbance to the other patients. Louisa heard Magda's tongue click disapprovingly as her hand trembled slightly through nerves as she withdrew the needle from the phial of medication. She *knew* that she was fumbling and inexperienced, but what she needed now was support, and not criticism.

After settling the man down, Magda tapped her way back into the office for a cup of tea, not bothering to ask Louisa if she'd like any, but she was past caring. She had been on her feet for hours—she only had the afternoon ward round to get through and then she was *off duty*! The

way she felt just now, she'd head straight for
bed!

She was bleeped by Sister in ICU, her voice
sounding anxious.

'Can you come at once please, Dr Gray?'

'But it's Dr Lloyd on call today,' Louisa protested, thinking of all the routine work she still
had to do.

'Yes, I know—but as it's Mrs Banks, whom
you admitted with Dr Forrester last night, he
thinks it best if you deal with it.'

'I'll be along,' said Louisa grudgingly. This
was Huw's job and he knew it. She was going
to have to assert herself with her senior house
officer before much longer, or else he was going
to completely walk all over her.

She arrived at the department to hear a man's
voice raised loud in anger, and a white-faced
Sister came hurrying over to meet her.

'Perhaps I'd better call Dr Forrester,' she said
quickly.

What had she just decided about asserting
herself? And she *was* the doctor now.

'Just a minute please, Sister.' She hardly
recognised the new, authoritative tone in her
voice. 'What exactly is the problem with Mrs
Banks? When I came by earlier, I was very
pleased with her progress. Has her condition
deteriorated?'

The Intensive Care Sister shook her head.
'She's fine. It's her husband who's causing the
problem—he's forced his way in here, shouting

abuse at her and insisting she accompanies him home. We've tried to stop her, but she's stated adamantly that she wants to go home with him. . . I. . .'

'I'll go and see her.' Louisa walked swiftly into the cubicle to find Mrs Banks holding weakly on to the side of the bed, nervously eyeing the burly giant who stood beside her.

Biting back an instinctive dislike, Louisa coolly met the hostile glare of Mr Banks. He stood at over six feet, and must have weighed two hundred pounds—his grubby T-shirt riding up over a huge expanse of beer belly. The expression in his curiously childlike pale blue eyes was distinctly unfriendly, and she wondered if the hand of Mr Banks was responsible for the fading black eye of his wife, or for the more sinister scar which snaked all the way down from her shoulder to her elbow.

She walked over to the bed and sat down, taking Mrs Banks' wrist in hers, and laying her fingers lightly on the pulse.

'You're not planning on leaving us just yet, are you?' she asked smilingly, and saw the look of indecision cross the other's face.

'Bloody right, she is,' butted in her husband. 'She wants to come 'ome to me and 'er kids.'

'I'm speaking to your wife,' said Louisa firmly. 'Perhaps you'd care to wait outside for a moment?'

He didn't budge, just stood there like some

immovable object, daring anyone to challenge him.

'I'd like to speak to your wife in private,' carried on Louisa, sounding much calmer than she actually felt. 'Just for a few minutes.'

'I'm not,' he said monotonously, 'going anywhere.'

Louisa thought quickly. Either she capitulated, or had Sister call up the hospital security guards, but either way the result would no doubt be the same.

She turned to the skinny woman still clutching on to the bed. 'What do *you* want to do, Mrs Banks?' she asked quietly.

'Go home,' she replied, in a tiny quavering voice.

'I have to tell you that I don't think that you should go home, not until you've seen a psychiatrist and a social worker.'

'Interfering cow,' muttered Mr Banks.

Louisa turned to face him. 'If you can't be quiet,' she said witheringly, 'then I shall have you thrown out.' She spoke again to his wife. 'Listen, Mrs Banks—if you are really determined to leave, then I can't force you to stay, but I have to tell you that you are discharging yourself against medical advice, and you must sign a form which states this. That means if you become ill as a result of your overdose, then we shan't be held responsible. Is that clear?'

Once again she saw the uncertainty in her

patient's face. Out of the corner of her eye she saw Mr Banks move forward menacingly.

'I'm leaving, Doctor.'

There remained only the form to be signed, the outpatient appointment with the psychiatrist to be given, which Louisa knew would be relegated to the pavement outside the hospital. The nurses helped Mrs Banks dress and she was assisted into a wheelchair.

Louisa stood back for a moment, watching the lift doors as they swung shut on the odd and sadly pathetic couple. The whole situation seemed so sordid, and she felt so powerless to help them. True, she had pumped Mrs Banks' stomach out, thus saving her from the overdose—but what had she done to alleviate the poverty and the hardship which was the cause of her original distress? What could any doctor do to make society more equal?

But there was little point in indulging in idealism. The very best she could do was to work well for her patients, to treat and diagnose them to the best of her ability. And the thought of diagnosis made her brighten up considerably. She still had Justin's Wolff-Parkinson-White's to announce at today's ward round. She hadn't had a chance to speak to Huw, but she presumed he would hand her back the ECG on the round itself.

She half ran over to Belling to arrive just as Adam and the team walked on to the ward. She felt slightly flummoxed by the pleasure she felt on sighting her boss, and more than a bit cross with herself for meeting his brief nod with a happy smile.

Huw was at the front of the notes trolley with Basil James as the white-coated team slowly made its way to each of their patients on the ward. When eventually they stopped before Justin's bed, to find him sitting up and smiling at them, Huw began to recite the case history and Louisa waited expectantly for him to give her a lead in. She could hardly believe what was to follow.

'Did you order an ECG?' asked Adam briskly.

The swarthy Welshman nodded complacently. 'Yes, sir. I have it here.'

'And what are your findings?'

'Well, sir——' Huw's voice was smug '—I'm pretty sure that the diagnosis is Wolff-Parkinson-White's.' He handed over the ECG for Adam to peruse.

Louisa felt sick as she watched them all agree with Huw, and noticed that not once had he dared to look in her direction. And he had told her not to even bother doing an ECG! She bit her lip with frustration, hurt and anger and looked up to find Adam's eyes on her.

She had to listen while Huw was praised for his quick thinking by Basil and to force her weary mind to concentrate on the rest of the cases. Just after five, when they had all drunk tea in the doctors' office on Dale ward, Adam left and she was able to make her escape, wanting to tackle Huw about his deception, but feeling that she might crumple and make a fool of herself in her present, tired state.

Outside, the relentless grey drizzle penetrated her white coat, seeping into the thick waves of her hair, until it started dripping coldly down her neck, no matter how she hurried.

The flat was very warm, and she crept into it, utterly exhausted, deciding to take a bath now rather than get in Adam's way later. She wondered how he was going to react when he learnt that she was not going to be moved elsewhere.

At least the bath brought a glow to her skin, and she dressed in a pair of jeans and a white cotton sweater—sitting before the bars of the electric fire in the sitting-room as she brushed her wet hair dry.

Hearing the door slam, she looked up, and Adam came into the room, catching his breath with surprise when he saw her crouched before the glowing orange bars.

'Louisa!' he exclaimed. 'Not moved out yet?'

Compared to the way he had spoken to her when she had first arrived, his words sounded like the honeyed tones of a diplomat, but the fatigue, tension and the stress of the past day made something inside her snap.

Clutching her damp towel to her breast, she opened her mouth to answer him, when to her horror she burst into uncontrollable noisy tears.

CHAPTER SEVEN

'Yes!' she sobbed. 'I *am* still here—and I'm here to stay, and so you'll just have to bloody well put up with it—my tights dripping in the bathroom, and lipstick on the cups and all the other things you think I'm going to do which are supposedly going to threaten your precious existence.' She finished on a gulp, wiping away with her fist the tears which refused to stop.

'Oh, God,' he muttered distractedly. 'Please don't, Louisa. Please don't cry—I didn't mean to make you cry.' He put his hand out towards her shoulder in a hesitant gesture of friendliness, but she pushed it away.

The tears continued to pour down her cheeks, and her breath was coming in juddering little gasps. It was bad enough that she was making the most awful fool of herself, without him standing there witnessing it.

'Go away,' she told him in a choked voice. 'Leave me alone.'

She was aware that he stood there for a few seconds longer before taking her at her word and walking out of the room, and his departure seemed to open the floodgates for a renewed bout of crying.

But she was not crying over Huw's childish

deception, or Adam's unfriendly behaviour towards her, or even because she was so mentally and physically exhausted that she no longer had any proper control over her feelings—although all these things had contributed. The tears that she cried were over a grief which went much deeper—a grief which she had kept locked up inside her for so long, tears she had never cried for Mike, or for the end of her marriage, healing tears she should never have suppressed.

She cried until she felt quite empty, until the shuddering of her breathing began to return gradually to normal, and she opened reddened hot eyes to find Adam kneeling on the floor in front of her, a glass of something in his hand which he gave to her.

'What is it?' she asked in between a sniff.

'Just fruit juice, I'm afraid there's nothing else—and besides, you don't seem terribly good at handling alcohol.'

She decided to ignore that, just took the glass and drank the juice gratefully, and its natural sweetness revived her, reminding her of how blotchy and ridiculous she must appear.

But Adam was still staring at her anxiously. 'Is that better?' he asked, and she nodded.

'I'm so sorry,' he said again.

A contrite Adam Forrester made a not unattractive picture, and was certainly a vast improvement on the surly version, but she couldn't let him shoulder all the blame for a distress which in reality had little to do with him.

'It doesn't matter,' she said wearily. 'I'm just overtired, that's all. Just leave me alone and I'll be all right.'

But he didn't leave her alone, he continued to kneel before her, his long limbs making her feel tiny by comparison. He seemed at a loss for words and she wished miserably that he would go. Her rage had been spent, and she felt like curling up in a corner on her own, like a little cat. She had railed at him, but his words had simply been the catalyst which had sparked off her outburst, and she had no intention of revealing to him the true reason for her tears.

'Listen to me, Louisa.' The deep voice was very soft. 'We haven't got off to a very good start, you and I, have we?'

She almost managed a smile as she shook her head. 'A slight piece of understatement!'

'It's been my fault, and I'm sorry—I've been foul to you, utterly foul. That evening when I came across you in the car park was the culmination of probably the worst weekend of my life—I guess that's why I overreacted the way I did. And then, when I arrived back home to find you ensconced here—looking as if you owned the place—that did it! I had no idea you were coming to live here, and I have to be honest—I don't particularly want to share with anyone—let alone a woman.'

His tone was wry and she wondered if Adam

Forrester were simply a misogynist, or whether he'd had an awful flatmate in the past. But she offered no comment, merely fixed her gaze steadily on him to hear what else he had to say.

'But if the powers that be decree that this is where you must live—then so be it! I bow my head in acceptance! And I apologise again.'

This time she did smile. She felt mollified by his apology, and relieved as well. As long as they could live in relative harmony she would be perfectly satisfied—the last thing she had wanted was for there to be some cloying, claustrophobic feud which had arisen, seemingly out of nothing. She wondered just what had happened to make it the 'worst weekend of my life'.

'One other thing,' he said quietly, shifting his position slightly. 'I was aware that it was you who made the diagnosis on Justin de Havilland, and not Huw.'

'How?' she asked, meeting the ice-blue eyes with interest.

He shrugged. 'Simple. Firstly, the expression on your face. Secondly, I know Huw and his capabilities. And lastly, I happened to catch a glimpse of the ECG in question when I woke you up in the middle of the night.'

She let her gaze fall, reluctant to let him see her blush again.

'And did you say anything to Huw?' she queried.

'No, I thought you'd probably want a quiet word with him yourself. Huw's basically a nice bloke—but he does the minimum to get by, and he'll take advantage if you let him, try it on even more if you're a woman, I expect.'

'Surprise, surprise,' she remarked acidly, and saw him look up sharply.

'Maybe it's going to be good having you around, Dr Louisa Gray! Already you've made me re-evaluate my attitude to women doctors—I always thought that all this business about not being treated as equals was an invention of overactive female brains—I can see that I may have been wrong!' He extended his hand and she placed hers in it, aware of the firm pressure of his grasp.

'Can we be friends as well as colleagues?' he asked.

She returned his smile with a broad grin of her own and nodded.

'I'd like that,' she agreed. 'I'd like that very much.'

Overnight, things changed for Louisa. Adam Forrester was as good as his word—the devil was banished and he became an angel, to use Mrs Jefferson's words. Not that she saw very much of him at home, contact was mainly on the wards or in Outpatients during their working day.

She did have a quiet word with Huw, and told him politely but firmly that she did not expect to have to cover his on call so that he could attend social or sporting engagements. He made a flustered excuse for having taken the credit for diagnosing Justin, claiming that he had simply forgotten to mention that it had been her ECG until it was too late. She accepted the apology with good grace, but inwardly made a resolution to tread warily with him in the future.

And Adam became her mentor and her teacher. Under his guidance and tuition her doctoring skills began to grow, so that as each day passed she became more and more proficient. He taught her things which were never written down satisfactorily in textbooks—ways to examine thoroughly, how to concentrate on the most important presenting factors in a case and not get bogged down by misleading signs. Occasionally, he showed her some wise shortcuts. He was kind and he was fair—if firm. When she made a mistake, he told her, but never with glee or remonstrance. Each mistake was a lesson, he advised her one morning as she glumly surveyed a test-tube full of clotted blood, and she should learn from it.

As she became more experienced, she needed him to accompany her less and less during their nights on call, so that she only had him bleeped if there was a crisis which she felt she was still too inexperienced to deal with.

At home she rarely saw him. He was a busy man. Apart from standing in for the absent consultant, he had his research. Masses of letters and periodicals arrived in the post for him each day and Louisa, with her few letters from her aunt and her friend Megan, often marvelled at his popularity. She knew that a lot of the correspondence was to do with the book and the papers he had written, and he was often asked for quotes by popular magazines and radio programmes. For someone who was quite a 'celebrity' in the medical world, he seemed remarkably free of conceit or affectation, she thought. She borrowed one of his papers from the library and was mesmerised. Erudite and informative, it nevertheless read as easily as a favourite novel.

She couldn't deny to herself that she found him quite spectacularly attractive. If circumstances had been different, he might have been a man she'd have liked to have dated. . .if only she weren't a walking disaster where men were concerned—and if only he'd shown the remotest indication that he felt likewise!

Left to her own devices, she built up a life of her own outside the confines of work. She joined the hospital photographic club, started playing badminton again and made friends with Mandy Patterson. The attractive, bespectacled ward sister had been at St Dunstan's since she was a student nurse, and seemed to know everyone who worked there. She introduced Louisa to a wide selection of staff, from doctors and nurses to porters and medical secretarial staff, and Louisa was gratified to get to know more people.

They often went shopping together. For the first time in her life, Louisa actually had some money and the freedom to choose how she spent it. Her childhood had not allowed for much in the way of pocket-money, and it had been the same at medical school—surviving on a meagre grant and then inheriting Mike's debts.

And now that there was money to spend, she didn't go mad—but it made a pleasant change to be able to purchase some clothes without having to scour the sales. With her first pay-cheque she bought two angora sweaters in fluffy shades of peach and cream, a short skirt in charcoal, several extravagantly frilly pieces of underwear, and a pale, pale grey dress in softest wool which clung to her body like a second skin and which she couldn't resist.

One night she went to a film with Mandy— an Oscar front runner starring Robert de Niro, whom they both admired. Afterwards they ate hamburgers at Bootsie's in the town, and went back to Mandy's flat in the Nurses' Home, where she insisted on them having a glass of Tia Maria.

'Here we are,' she giggled, as she carefully tipped the sweet brown liqueur into minute tumblers. 'I must finish this bottle off before Christmas—an ex-patient of ours brings me a new one every Christmas Eve.'

'Sounds good,' said Louisa, taking a sip.

Mandy put her glass down carefully on the

bookcase and surveyed Louisa curiously. 'Mind if I ask you something?'

Louisa grinned. 'Asked away. You want to know why I've switched Mr Fisher over to Septrin from flucoxacillin?'

'Nothing as prosaic as that!' protested Mandy. 'I'm just interested to know what it's like living with the great man?'

'You mean Adam?'

'Well, I don't mean the man in the moon, that's for sure!'

Louisa thought for a moment. 'Of course, it's not strictly accurate to say we're living together. We're just sharing the same flat!' she teased.

Mandy ignored that. 'Is he very different— out of work?'

What *was* he really like? It was a question she had been asking herself for weeks now.

'He's a very unusual man,' she said finally. 'I know he's got a temper, because I saw it when I first arrived, but since then he's been as nice as can be—charming, helpful, witty. I don't actually see that much of him, because he works very hard and plays a lot of sport.'

There was silence for a moment. He was the most private person she had ever met and she was suddenly reminded of a wooden Chinese doll she had been given as a child—the doll was in two halves and you could pull them apart to reveal another version of the same doll underneath.

'I think he keeps the real Adam Forrester

hidden deep away inside him—I don't think he lets anyone get very close to him.'

Mandy nodded. 'You know he was married, don't you?'

Louisa stiffened, her attention now unwavering. She should not have been surprised—he was, after all, almost thirty-five years old, talented and good-looking to boot. It made her realise that they all kept little bits of themselves hidden from the world—she had told no one here that she herself had been married.

'No,' she said quietly. 'I didn't know.'

Mandy was no great gossip, but she settled back happily in her chair, filled with the very natural human pleasure at being able to impart information.

'Oh, yes! She was terribly rich—some industrialist's daughter, the father was dead against the marriage. And he was right—it lasted under a year before she left him. It even made the national press. Let me see, I think I've still got the piece somewhere.'

She got up and began scrabbling around in the paper-filled drawer of a small bureau.

Louisa raised her eyebrows. 'You *kept* the article?'

'I know.' Mandy's voice sounded abashed. 'Silly, isn't it? I've had a crush on him for years, it's no secret. So has Magda.' She handed Louisa a rather crumpled-looking newspaper clipping.

'But neither of you have ever been out with him?'

Mandy's smile was wide, but her eyes were sad. 'You're joking. He doesn't even notice we exist—he doesn't go out with anyone from work. We reckon he's still in love with *her*.' She nodded quite viciously towards the item.

Louisa looked down at it with interest. It was from one of the upmarket tabloids and fairly typical. It showed a wedding day picture, dramatically torn apart, with the headline 'A Rift Which Would Not Heal.' The photo showed Adam in morning suit, smiling crookedly, his dark hair slightly ruffled, an arm round the silk-clad shoulders of his bride. The girl with him was quite exquisitely lovely—her hair a bright golden bell which fell to her shoulders, wide eyes and a rather aristocratic nose. It read:

It seems that Daddy was right! Just eleven months after their fashionable Westminster wedding, heiress Clara Walker, 21, and her doctor husband Adam Forrester, 33, are separating.

Violently opposed to the marriage between his only child and television personality Forrester, Sir John Walker was a noticeable absentee from the St Valentine's Day service. He was unavailable today for comment.

Friends of the couple say the parting has been 'amicable'.

'That was about two years ago,' said Mandy quietly. 'Doesn't he ever talk about her?'

Louisa shook her head slowly. No wonder he

was such a private man, if the whole hospital knew all about his affairs. 'No,' she replied. 'He's never said a word.'

But she knew in her heart of hearts that if he had confided in her, that she would not have told anyone else about it, not even someone she liked as much as Mandy Patterson.

'Are you. . .?' Mandy's voice sounded tentative. 'Do you like him, too?'

'Not in the way that you mean,' said Louisa firmly. 'I like him as a flatmate and a colleague, and that's all. Don't forget I've only just started my first house job. I'm just beginning my career—I haven't any time for men! And even if I did, the last person I'd choose would be a doctor!'

It was true, she thought as she walked home, hugging her navy coat closer to her against the chill wind. She hadn't ruled out the possibility that one day she might marry again, somewhere in that indistinct haze known as the future. But any partner would need to be solid and supportive, with regular hours of his own, to balance her crazy ones. Perhaps a stockbroker, or a solicitor. A relationship with two doctors in the house was doomed to failure—two lots of irregular hours meant that you never saw each other!

She smiled as she turned the key in the lock. That was the first sign of old age, wasn't it? When you started becoming fanciful!

Discover Masquerade

WITH 2 FREE BOOKS

Masquerade historical romances bring the past alive with splendour, excitement and romance. As a special introductory offer we will send you 2 Masquerade romances together with a cuddly teddy bear and a surprise mystery gift - completely FREE.

We will also reserve a subscription for you which means you could go on to enjoy four more exciting new books, delivered to your door before they're available in the shops, every two months for just £1.75 each - postage and packing FREE. Plus a FREE newsletter giving you information on the top authors, competitions, (our last lucky winner won £600!), and much more.

What's more there are no strings attached, you can stop receiving books at any time, so don't delay, complete and return this card NOW!

Complete the coupon overleaf.

FREE BOOKS COUPON

Fill in the coupon now!

Yes! Please send me 2 FREE Masquerade romances together with my FREE teddy and mystery gift and reserve a subscription for me. If I decide to subscribe I shall receive 4 new Masquerade titles every two months for £7.00, postage and packing FREE. If I decide not to subscribe I shall write to you within 10 days. The FREE books and gifts are mine to keep in any case. I understand that I can cancel or suspend my subscription at any time simply by writing to you. I am over 18 years of age.

Free Gift

Mystery Gift

6AOM

Name _____

Address _____

_____ Postcode _____

Signature _____
(I am over 18 years age.)

Send no money now - take no risks

NO STAMP NEEDED

Reader Service
FREEPOST
P.O. Box 236
Croydon
Surrey
CR9 9EL

CHAPTER EIGHT

OCTOBER melted into November and the snow
fell fiercely and blocked roads and froze pipes
with her icy mantle. Louisa, used to the more
temperate climes of the south, found that she
needed to wear extra layers of clothing to coun-
teract the cold.

Justin de Havilland, her patient with the
Wolff-Parkinson-White's, had been discharged
home with advice and drugs, and seemed eter-
nally grateful to her. Louisa was sorry to see
him go, for she had become fond of him.

He reappeared in Outpatients one day and
shook her hand.

'I want to thank you again, Dr Gray,' he said.

'You've thanked me enough already, Justin,'
she protested. 'And anyway, I didn't really do
anything—if I hadn't found out what was the
matter with you, then someone else would have
done.'

The exotic creature shook his head so that the
dark curls flew round his pale face. 'You listened
to me. You didn't prejudge because of my
family's position, or because of my
slightly. . .er. . .unusual appearance.'

She couldn't help laughing.

'Anyway,' he finished shyly, 'I've done this

for you—I hope you like it. It's with all my love.'

He thrust a large manilla envelope into her hand and hurried away, his gold-threaded overcoat swirling around him, and she could almost have sworn that he was blushing.

Adam had been next door consoling a relative and walked in just as she was sliding her fingernail under the flap. Inside was a thick sheet of white cartridge paper.

It was a portrait done in the soft, smudgy medium of charcoal, and it was of Louisa, though she hardly recognised it at first—surely that beautiful, solemn-eyed creature could not be her? The cheekbones looked higher and finer than her own, and the lips more sultry and chiselled. And how, by the use of a single piece of burnt wood, had he managed to make her hair look so gleaming and lustrous?

'It's very lovely,' said Adam, looking over her shoulder.

'He's embellished it, of course,' smiled Louisa, putting it carefully back in its envelope.

'Don't you believe it,' said Adam, very softly, and something in his voice, something in the expression in his eyes sent a shiver running through her body and she turned away to put the envelope in the drawer of a desk until the clinic was over.

The nurse appeared with the next patient, and Louisa had to swallow three or four times in quick succession to try to calm her racing heart.

What the hell was the matter with her? Did she intend to imitate Mandy, and Magda, and goodness knows how many others, by falling for a man who was still in love with his ex-wife?

It was a relief when the patient was helped up on to the trolley, and she could watch as Adam leant over and gently tapped her chest and back, and then listened to her heart sounds with his stethoscope. She stood by the middle-aged woman's side and gave her what she hoped was a comforting grin.

After Adam had finished, he stood up. 'Have a listen now, will you, Louisa? Tell me what you can hear.'

This was the part that she had hated at first. As a student you got to listen to very few heart sounds, so that as a newly qualified doctor she had felt totally incapable of ever diagnosing any cardiac disorder. And the worst thing was that the moment you donned a white coat, then every nurse in the hospital seemed to think you were an expert on *everything*! The heart sounds were the worst because the differences between normal and abnormal sounds were so slight. It needed a discerning ear to recognise the normal sounds, so subtle were the clicks and murmurs of valves opening and closing and blood emptying and filling the four chambers of this major vessel.

After about a week, Adam had seen her

worried expression before a ward round one morning, had asked what the problem was and she had told him. To her surprise he had merely laughed, told her her fears were normal, and had lent her a cassette tape which played all the normal and abnormal heart sounds. She had listened to it over and over, until one day it had all clicked into place, and since then she had rarely been wrong in recognising what she heard.

She placed the drum of her stethoscope on the woman's chest, rubbing it briskly with the palm of her hand first, so that the cold metal wouldn't startle her.

She listened carefully to the muted roaring of the heart, and when she had finished she could see Adam looking at her expectantly.

The nurse began to help the patient to dress, and Adam and Louisa walked slowly back into the office.

'So what's your diagnosis?' he queried.

She hesitated. She had heard a diastolic and systolic murmur, of that she was certain. Which meant only one sure diagnosis. The trouble being that this particular illness was now extremely uncommon, and it was rare enough to make her question her theory. So was she sure?

She met Adam's eyes confidently. 'I think she has mixed mitral disease,' she said in an undertone, and knew immediately from the flash of pleasure in his eyes that she had been right.

'You're going on heart sounds alone?'

'Mostly. But I got a chance to glance through her notes. The patient spent the first eighteen years of her life in a caravan on the west coast of Ireland, and from her description it sounds as though she had rheumatic fever as a child.'

He nodded. 'So what treatment would you advise, and what's the likely outcome?'

Her answer was fluent—she'd read up on this last week.

'Are you going to be my star pupil, Dr Gray?' he teased her and once again she was flummoxed by the disproportionate amount of pleasure and pride she felt under his obvious approbation. Did the foul-tempered man she had met on her first day at the hospital really exist—or had he just been a figment of her imagination?

She didn't know what was worse, really— feeling alienated by him, or starting to care for him in a way which was totally unprofessional. And the trouble with feeling the way that she was feeling right now, was that she was probably reading far more into his words and gestures than he intended. It was the classic master/ pupil relationship, she thought ruefully, where the novice begins to idolise his or her mentor.

Thank goodness Adam Forrester did not have the power to read her mind! Mrs O'Mara was summonsed back into the office and Louisa listened while he slowly and carefully explained the disease to her.

The rest of the clinic passed quickly, with Louisa fiercely concentrating on the work in hand, making a conscious effort not to let her attention stray to the dark, craggy profile as he wrote in the notes.

Then at five-fifteen, just as the last patient was being shown out, the phone rang and the nurse picked it up. A slightly puzzled frown crossed her face, and she covered the receiver with her hand and spoke to Adam.

'It's for you, Dr Forrester,' she said hesitantly.

'Who is it?' he asked, without looking up from the notes.

The nurse actually went pink around her ears. 'It's—er—I think it's a personal call.'

Something in the tone of her voice made him look up quickly and he took the instrument from her.

'Yes?'

It was ironic that Louisa had been wondering what had happened to the Mr Hyde side of his personality, for suddenly he had materialised in front of them. A look of helpless rage had crossed his face, and the blue eyes blazed with a look of anger which made her realise that his minor skirmish with her had been like a drop in the ocean in comparison to what she was seeing now.

His voice was icy. 'I thought I told you never to ring me at work?'

Louisa and the nurse looked at one another with mortified expressions, wondering how on earth they could extricate themselves without making it glaringly obvious that they could hear every word of the conversation. The nurse dashed over to the handbasin and began rinsing out a test-tube, and Louisa suddenly found a set of notes utterly absorbing. But it was impossible not to listen to what was being said.

'Have you? Have you really? Well, that's wonderful—let me be the first to congratulate you.' The sarcasm and the venom in his voice cut through the atmosphere like a laser, and for a moment Louisa shivered.

She could see the white of his knuckles where he held the receiver.

'No, *you* listen,' he was saying, and for a wild impetuous moment Louisa wished that she could run up and cradle him in her arms, to try to take some of the pain out of his voice. 'I happen to be in Outpatients, otherwise I'd be telling you more strongly, but since I can't give vent to my true feelings I'll put it as politely as possible—you can go to hell! Understand that?'

The person at the other end clearly had got the message, and Louisa assumed that the receiver had been slammed down for he was left standing there gazing rather blankly at the mouthpiece, before laying it carefully in its rest with an exaggeratedly slow movement, like a man suffering from shock.

Louisa had been wondering frantically what she was going to say to him, but she was saved the trouble.

'I'm sorry about that,' he said, in an unfamiliarly heavy voice. 'I just had some rather—some rather disturbing news. Thanks, Louisa. Thanks, nurse.' He nodded rather curtly to them both, and strode out of the office without another word, and they were left looking rather blankly at each other.

'I'll be going now, too,' said Louisa quickly. The last thing she wanted to encourage was a discussion about whom he had been talking to, and what the disturbing news had been. She hoped that this nurse was not a gossipy type, but she was frankly amazed at Adam being so indiscreet. Up until now, he had been the model of professional behaviour while at work. It must have been some news to have made him react like that.

'Thanks again for your help,' she said, closing the office door quietly shut behind her.

She didn't know what to do. If Adam had gone directly home, he might not want her around. In her own experience, people who had received bad news were better off coping with it privately. She had lived like a hermit after her bust-up with Mike.

She looked at her watch. It was now five-thirty and the doctors' bar was open. She could go and have a couple of drinks and find someone to chat to over there.

The bar was almost deserted, which wasn't really surprising when she considered how early it was. She bought herself an orange juice and lemonade, unable to face the thought of any alcohol so soon after the tea she'd drunk in the clinic.

Presently a couple of surgeons who she knew vaguely came in, and she was invited to make up a foursome playing pool at the other end of the room.

She thoroughly enjoyed herself—Daniel Betts had a particularly sharp sense of humour, and she found herself giggling more than once.

At seven she judged it safe to go home. Daniel and the other two men were planning to go for an Indian meal in the town and they tried to persuade her to go with them, but she declined the offer.

'I'm exhausted,' she explained. 'I was on call last night, and only managed to get about an hour's sleep. If I don't have an early night tonight, I'll be crawling to work tomorrow morning!'

James, the tall, thin surgeon with the rather angular features and pale eyes spoke. 'You're working with wonder boy, I take it?'

She wrinkled her nose, not comprehending. 'Wonder boy?'

'Our very own television star—Adam Forrester.'

'Yes, I am, and as a matter of fact he never mentions the show—it seems to me that other people are obsessed with his success, not him.' She was aware that she had immediately sprung to his defence; she caught a knowing look pass between the three men and could have kicked herself. They would have her down as yet another love-struck Forrester fan.

She walked slowly back to the flat, and as soon as she stepped into the hall she could see the light on in the sitting-room. She paused for a moment, unsure of whether to go in, but she couldn't just ignore him—and, what was more, she wanted to see him.

She found him stretched out on the floor, his long legs sprawled in front of him, his back against the sofa, a glass of wine by his side.

At the sound of her footsteps he looked up, such a vulnerable expression on his face that her heart went out to him. She had never imagined that he could be hurt, or wounded— the image did not match up to the ideal of the powerful, successful media star. Was she as guilty as all the others of not looking beyond the impressive exterior to the character of the true man underneath?

'Drinking on your own?' she said lightly.

He looked at her thoughtfully. 'Not necessarily. You could always get a glass and join me.'

Her knees were actually shaking—and all he had done was make the most casual of suggestions. If she was hoping for something more, then she was almost certainly going about it the wrong way. He was a man who was used to getting whatever he wanted—the only way to impress him would be not to fawn all over him like his legions of fans.

She hesitated, armed with some kind of instinctive foresight which told her that to accept his offer would change the whole balance of their now amicable relationship.

But her hesitation was as fleeting as a summer rainbow. He fascinated her as no man had ever fascinated her before, and she wanted to get to know him better—was that such a crime?

She wondered if his experience with women made him aware of what absurd, schoolgirlish thoughts were whirling around in her head as she smiled her acceptance.

'I'd love a drink!' she exclaimed. 'I thought you'd never ask!'

CHAPTER NINE

SHE fetched a glass from the sideboard, and throwing her white coat on to an armchair, sat down on the floor beside him. He filled her glass with wine and handed it to her.

She took a sip. 'Thanks. Are you celebrating—or drowning your sorrows?' she suggested.

There was the glimmer of a smile. 'Very tactful,' he remarked. 'Are you trying to tell me that you didn't overhear my telephone conversation?'

She took another sip. 'I was certainly trying my best not to—but you know how small the room is.'

He sighed. 'I shouldn't have lost my temper.'

There was a momentary silence. She didn't know quite what to say—she wanted to help, but she didn't want to pry.

He was staring at her, the narrow eyes faintly amused.

'Well? Aren't you going to ask me about it?'

She looked at him calmly. 'What?'

'The phone call. Why I'm sitting here quietly getting drunk at seven o'clock in the evening?'

She shrugged. 'It's none of my business, is it? If you want to tell me about it, you will. It's not my place to pry.'

He raised his eyebrows, clearly surprised. 'A woman lacking the natural curiosity of her sex? How very odd.'

She returned his gaze coolly, remembering when he'd mistaken her for a nurse. 'You still make a lot of assumptions about women, don't you, Adam?'

'Do I? Perhaps I do. Maybe you're the first woman that I've met who doesn't want to hear my life story within the first five minutes of knowing me.'

Coming from him that almost sounded like a compliment, she thought, wondering how it was possible to be so calm and unflappable with him while inside her stomach was tying itself up in knots.

'That wasn't what you thought on the night we first met,' she reminded him. 'You said that I was an empty vessel, making a lot of noise!'

He laughed. 'Did I? How absolutely insufferable! That must rate as my worst character assessment of all time.'

Stop it, she told herself furiously. He doesn't *mean* anything by it. But that didn't stop her eyes shining at his words, or her next remark.

'I just want to say that I'm around if you need me, Adam. If you want to talk—that's fine, but if you don't, well, that's fine too. Sometimes it's better to talk about things, and doctors are notoriously bad about listening to other people's problems and then bottling their own up.'

A smile creased his craggy features. 'This

sounds like a psychiatrist in the making!' There was a long pause. 'I'm sitting drowning my sorrows because I feel a spectacular failure, if you really want to know. And I don't like to fail.'

She couldn't keep the surprise out of her voice. 'You! A failure! What rubbish!'

'I'm flattered that you should find it such an inappropriate description! Why am I talking rubbish?'

'Because you're well-known in your field—and you've written all those books and papers. You've got a job you obviously adore, you're a good doctor—and what's more—the patients all love you!'

He looked at her consideringly, a suggestion of a smile playing on his lips. 'That's a very sweet thing to say, Louisa. Very loyal, and very sweet.'

'But it's not,' she protested vehemently. 'It's true, every word of it—and if you consider yourself a failure, then where does that put the rest of us?'

'My divorce became finalised today,' he said slowly, refilling his glass.

'And my ex-wife, with her impeccable sense of timing, chose today to announce the fact that she intends to marry the producer of Here's Health. She also expects me to be overjoyed about her pregnancy, conveniently forgetting that she had always told me she wanted no children. All in all, some wonderful news, wasn't it?' he asked sarcastically.

She said nothing, just sat watching him and waiting, trying to blot out the irrational jealousy that another woman should be able to make him feel so much. Mandy was right—he must still be in love with her.

'Maybe you're right—perhaps I should talk about it.' He spoke almost as though she were not there, and still she said nothing.

'I kind of fell into the whole television thing,' he explained. 'It wasn't something that I had planned. I wrote the book, and a few papers, and that snowballed and I found I was being asked to write more and more. Then there was all that ridiculous fuss about the watercress. . .'

'I remember,' she interposed, taking a mouthful of the rich, red wine.

'At first it seemed the most incredibly good fortune. I could continue with my research while working on the programme. And I thought. . .' He shrugged his shoulders with an almost boyish bashfulness. 'Naïvely thought, I suppose—that here was a chance to educate the public on health, to change ways of thinking. A pioneer programme in preventative medicine was what I envisaged.'

'And wasn't it?'

He shook his head. 'Not at all. Oh, it's all been done since, I know. But all they wanted then was a variation on the watercress story—just gimmicks and bizarre medical problems.

That's why I only stuck it for two series. And that's where I met my wife,' he added. 'Correction, my *ex*-wife.'

She found herself flinching at the pain in his face, wanting again to reach out and comfort him.

'It turned out that she was a friend of my producer. A very *good* friend, it transpired,' he added bitterly. 'But I was the "star". It was the star she wanted, the star she must have, and I was foolish enough to be dazzled by her youth, and her beauty and the careless charm which comes from having everything in life you've always wanted.'

Why did it hurt so much to hear him talk this way, she thought desperately, taking another sip of wine in an effort to detract from her confusion.

'She thought she'd married a television star—what she failed to realise was that she'd married a doctor.'

He stared into the distance. 'The trouble started when I gave up the show and became a humble registrar. Clara simply couldn't understand that I had to work nights. And weekends. That I had a job which carried an enormous responsibility, and that, to do it well, I had to work hard. It didn't take long after that for things to completely fall apart. If I was on call for the weekend and there happened to be a party in London—then she would go on her own. Marriage can't survive separate lives, and ours was no exception. . .'

He cleared his throat and looked at her. 'I'm sorry, Louisa. I've talked and talked, and about myself, too—I've been boring you.'

There was nothing remotely boring about this man, she decided as she shook her head. Nothing at all. 'No, you're not,' she said very gently, and then, momentarily embarrassed, she reached out for her glass at exactly the same moment as he did and as their hands brushed together they looked at one another, startled.

Was it the contact of his skin against hers, or their proximity? whispered a voice in her head as she instantly became aware that something had happened—the whole atmosphere in the room had changed—charged up as if by electricity.

And he was staring at her with an expression on his face which she couldn't for the life of her work out.

'Louisa. . .'

Whether the word was a command or an entreaty she could not tell; all she knew was that she was powerless to stop the tantalisingly slow movement of his head as he bent to kiss her.

His arms went round her and he pulled her to the floor, and as their lips met and fused in a bruising collision she felt his mouth part to greet hers in a fierce kind of sensual ownership.

Her body seemed to melt and mingle with

his. She could feel his heart pounding against her breast and it seemed like the most gloriously intimate sensation in the world, sending shivers of delight to every sensitive nerve ending in her body.

But reason began to return, seeping into her numbed brain like cold water, sending her body into a silent yearning protest as she moved fractionally away from him.

Because she wanted him, yes, but not like this. Not when he'd been drinking, when the wine might be orchestrating his movements. And to let him make love to her now would link her indelibly in his mind with his ex-wife, whom he'd spent the whole evening talking about. The day that his marriage had ended was no day to start something new. If Adam Forrester wanted her, then he must want her for herself alone, not as someone to provide comfort, or, worse still—as a substitute.

He felt the change in her immediately and sat up, pushing back the ruffled dark hair from his forehead in an achingly attractive gesture which made her long to feel the closeness of his body against her body, the touch of his mouth against her mouth.

'Hell. . .' he muttered, jumping to his feet. 'Forgive me—I guess it was reflex action.'

Reflex action! If that was what happened with reflex action, what on earth must it be like when he kissed you with seduction in mind?

To her astonishment and dismay, he seemed

completely unaffected by the kiss which had knocked her for six. Was she reading something into it, which had simply been invented by an impressionable woman who was half in love with her boss?

She rose to her feet shakily, scarcely able to look him in the eyes, but he put his hands on her shoulders and she caught her breath, thinking that he was about to repeat the embrace.

'That's no way for friends to act, is it?' he asked teasingly, and she willed her face not to show her disappointment as she shook her head in agreement.

'And besides—sex always complicates things, doesn't it? Mmm?'

Well, she certainly couldn't argue with that. She nodded, suddenly realising that she hadn't spoken one word back to him. How shaming that he could have aroused her to such a pitch so easily.

'Are you all right?' She hated the new concern in his voice, as if he was now in the presence of someone he didn't really know very well.

'Yes, I'm fine,' she said brightly, wishing that he would just go. 'Let's forget it ever happened.'

He smiled. 'You're a honey, Louisa. A real pal.' And then his face was serious once more. 'Thanks for listening. I'm very grateful.' He glanced at the watch on his wrist. 'Heavens! Is that the time? I'd better go out for a run—work off some of that wine, not to mention some of my—er—aggression.'

She watched him go. There was no doubt in her mind that he was embarrassed by what had just occurred; she had never seen him so stilted, so formal.

She retreated to her room, listening to him moving around in his, half of her longing to obliterate the memory, while the rest of her went over it, detail by glorious detail.

Because his kiss had woken in her some nebulous promise of fulfilment, had left her body aching and hungry; more than that—it had carved a place for him in her heart.

She had spent the past few years deliberately erecting barriers around her battered heart—high fences through which no man would ever pass.

And by one simple action Adam Forrester had carelessly knocked them all aside, had unforgettably, irrevocably permeated her whole being and left her weak with longing for him.

How ever was she going to be able to face him?

CHAPTER TEN

IT SOON became clear to Louisa that she was going to have little difficulty facing Adam, because he was going out of his way to avoid her. He might as well have moved out of the flat, she saw him there so infrequently. He started playing a prodigious amount of sport, often appearing late in the evening, his long brown legs contrasting against the snowy whiteness of his shorts, the dark hair damply curling around his neck.

She saw him at work, of course, but an air of constraint had marred their earlier, easier companionship and she mourned its loss. She was delighted to hear from Mandy that Dr Fenton-Taylor was due back from America and would resume work in the hospital just before Christmas. At least then Adam would return to his research post and she would be spared the awkwardness of daily contact with him.

At times she wondered which had caused him the greater embarrassment—kissing her, or having taken her into his confidence. She suspected that it was most probably the latter, because it was obvious that he had kissed a good few girls in his time—and she couldn't imagine for a moment that he'd be unable to cope with something like that!

But essentially he was such a private man that he was probably rueing the day when wine had loosened his tongue enough to tell his house officer all about the break up of his marriage.

Well, he needn't fear anything from her. She had no intention of breathing a word to a soul about what he had said. Perhaps she should simply confront him and tell him his secrets were safe with her, but how could she when he almost ran a mile every time he saw her? And in a way it was a relief to be spared contact with him, because she was discovering things about herself all the time, and one of them was that she was finding it increasingly difficult to behave normally when he was around.

She had never before felt the self-consciousness of the infatuated. When he walked into a room she could see only him, and when he stood beside her she felt an overpowering desire to touch him. Sometimes at night she would lie awake, fantasising that he would come to her room, late one night. . .

He never did, of course. He remained at all times urbane and professional, the familiar stranger. Time and time again she would glance at the calendar on the wall of her small room. Four weeks to go until Christmas and then just eight short weeks after that she would be far away from St Dunstan's and the disturbingly powerful charms of Dr Adam Forrester.

Sometimes, when she should have been studying, she would sit at her small desk staring out at the bare knotted branches of an oak silhouetted against a sky of sulphur—wishing that all could be at peace in her world again.

She received confirmation from St Bartholomew's that her surgical house job had been arranged at St Agnes's, a large district general hospital which was over fifty miles away from St Dunstan's.

But then something happened which put all thoughts of Adam Forrester out of her mind.

She had been asked by Basil, her registrar, to have a quick look at a young girl who had drunk three quarters of a bottle of whisky and who was in a sorry state in one of the cubicles in Casualty.

The girl was only fifteen, and had been violently sick of her own accord, so at least there was no need to perform a stomach wash-out on her.

Louisa turned to Sister Hindmarsh. 'I don't want to admit her, but as the department's quiet—could we put her in one of the cubicles for a couple of hours to observe her?'

'I'll see to it right away,' replied the obliging Casualty sister.

Louisa was on her way to the office, passing through the waiting-room when she started, recognising a thick-set man sitting cradling a small boy, but unable to remember where she knew him from.

Intrigued, she stood for a moment watching him and as his pale, rather childish eyes met hers, she had instant recall and quickly carried on through to the office. The last time she had seen him he'd been looking menacing in the Intensive Care Unit, frogmarching his wife out against medical advice. What was his name, now?

Banks! That was it. And the small boy must be his son. She remembered stooping to pick up the battered photograph of him which had fluttered out of Mrs Banks' handbag on to the floor.

The Casualty Officer was seated at the desk, and she leaned over him to scan the admissions book, but try as she might, she could find no one under the name of 'Banks'.

'There's a toddler in the waiting-room, with his father. Do you know what he's in for?'

Sister frowned in concentration. 'Toddler? Oh, yes—that'll be Darren Watts. Poor little fellow took a tumble downstairs.'

Louisa frowned. She would be prepared to swear on her life that the child was Bobby Banks, but what if she was wrong?

Why should the father lie about his son's name? Unless. . .unless the name of Bobby Banks was already known in the department. It was just a hunch, but. . .

'Do you have an NAI book?' she asked.

Sister Hindmarsh looked curious. 'Yes, we do.'

'Mind if I take a look at it?'

'Help yourself.' Sister selected a small black volume from the shelf above the desk and handed it to Louisa.

NAI was short for non-accidental injury, the medical term for what was commonly known as child abuse. Any child presented at the department with an injury which staff suspected had been administered violently was monitored in a book, so that extra care would be taken while examining them on subsequent visits to the department. And of course, if a record was kept, then the Social Services department would have proof of abuse, and this would facilitate the child's being taken into care if need be.

Louisa ran her finger down page after page of entries, until she found what she was looking for. There it was, in black and white, dated the previous summer when he was only seventeen months old.

'BANKS Bobby (17 mths). Ingested Stemitil suppository. Black eye and laceration to left cheek noted. Mother claimed injuries inflicted by older sister.'

Sister Hindmarsh was observing her silently. 'What's up?' she asked.

Louisa recited the facts as briefly as she could and saw a frown appear on the older woman's face.

'You're quite sure it's the same boy?'

'I'm positive.'

Sister turned to the Casualty Officer, who had been sitting taking it all in. 'What do you reckon we should do?'

He thought for a moment. 'Well, we can't ignore it, obviously. But there again, we don't want to make the father suspicious, or he might simply take the child and do a runner—and not only will we have missed being able to help, but the little fellow won't get his head injury attended to.'

He tapped his pen on the blotter before him. 'I think the best thing is if we take him up to X-ray accompanied by a nurse, rather than the father—and while he's up there we'll do a full skeletal X-ray. I'll ring up the duty paediatrician and find out more. It's more his province, really.'

'I'll get a nurse,' said Sister briskly, and Louisa caught her by the arm.

'Could I go up with him, as well?'

Sister looked doubtful and glanced over to the Casualty Officer, who shrugged slightly.

'Very well. If you're sure you want to.'

Louisa nodded. 'I want to.'

She found a teddy bear in a cupboard outside the office and put it in the child's arms as he was wheeled on the narrow trolley towards the lift. She looked at him closely, at the thin scrawny body, the threadbare clothes, and the muddy mark over a fading scar on his cheek. She should have been off duty by now, but in a strange kind of way she felt responsible for him.

And if she was proved right, then she would have helped him.

For a moment she clenched her fists inside the pockets of her white coat, trying to quash the strong sense of injustice she felt about a boy of not yet three who had been subjected to so much misery in his short life. But she knew that, however horrendous and distasteful the medical profession found these types of injury, that it was not their job to sit in judgement, but to offer help and support, in an attempt to defuse potentially explosive situations. And she also knew that an abused child was just like any other in that it loved its parents.

The boy was drowsy, and she instinctively smoothed back a lock of filthy blond hair which flopped on to his forehead.

In X-ray, she donned a lead apron to block out the dangerous rays, and watched as the radiographer took films of the child's skull, arms, legs, torso, abdomen and cervical spine. She asked Louisa to wait outside while she developed them.

The staff nurse from Casualty stood by the desk chatting animatedly to one of the radiographers whom she evidently knew quite well, and Louisa just sat holding the hand of the small, pathetic figure on the trolley.

She wondered why she felt such a bond with him, this child alone. She thought back to her own childhood. Another child alone. Aunt Beatrice had tried very hard, but she had not loved her, not *really* loved her in the way that her mother had done. And a child could be very sensitive to duty disguised as love. Could her loveless childhood have been in part responsible for her impetuous marriage—had she grasped at the first person, because he had seemed to offer her the one thing which had been missing from her life?

The radiographer walked out of the dark-room, the newly developed films in her hand, her face serious.

'I'm just going to ask the radiologist to report on these,' she told Louisa gravely.

It seemed that Louisa's fears and instincts had been correct—the small boy showed an old fracture scar on his right humerus, one which the radiologist read as being caused by the arm being twisted.

Louisa bit her lip, her heart going out to the young boy. But she knew that the abusers of children were often the victims of abuse them-selves, and that poverty and low intelligence all were contributors to a situation where the father was little more than a child himself, and who reacted to stress as a child would—by hitting out blindly and irrationally.

The duty paediatrician was bleeped, a young South African whom Louisa knew through Mandy.

'What will happen to him now, Mark?' she asked.

'I want to admit him anyway,' he replied

slowly. 'Because of the head injury. And then I'm going to speak to the social worker. I think we'll probably make a place-of-safety order—we can't take any more risks. I'll go down and have a word with Mr Banks.' His serious young face softened for a moment.

'I gather it was you who noticed that the father had lied about the child's name. Thanks very much for being so observant. Hopefully, we'll be able to put the whole family into therapy—sort the problem out and stop it from happening again.'

'Thanks,' she replied. 'I hope I did the right thing.'

She gave Bobby's hand a final squeeze and caught the lift down to the ground floor. Six o'clock. Adam should have left for whichever game of sport had claimed him this evening. Thank goodness she had arranged to go into Dunchester with Mandy this evening. It was late night closing and a new boutique had opened last week. She had just been paid, too, and the way she was feeling she'd like to blow all her wages in an effort to dispel the cloying frustration she felt!

She was idly kicking a pebble along the path towards her flat, when a blast of cold air chilled her and she pushed her hands deep into her pocket to discover that her stethoscope was missing.

Drat! What had she done with it? She tried to remember where she'd been before she took

Bobby up to X-ray. She had last used it to listen to the heart of the fifteen-year-old who had drunk the whisky. Turning around, she began walking briskly towards Casualty.

It was unusually deserted, and she heard an angry shouting somewhere in the distance, then her heart sank as she saw the massive bulk of Mr Banks accompanied by a porter, heading down the corridor towards her.

Little hairs stood up on the back of her head and began to prickle. She knew he'd seen her and panic flared up in her throat, making it difficult to breathe.

He approached, looming towards her as solid as a mountain, and as he grew closer she was caught in the field of a stare which contained nothing but hatred. He stopped, blocking her path.

'It was *you*, wasn't it—you bitch?' The porter held up a restraining hand, but he pushed it away, while moving his face closer to Louisa's so that she recoiled from the malevolence there.

Fear had paralysed her. She opened her mouth to ask him to move, but her vocal cords had been rendered unusable, and only a meaningless croak emerged.

'Mr Banks!' The large West Indian porter had raised his voice threateningly. 'If you don't move it, then I'm calling the police.'

The arm of the porter propelled him forwards,

but not before he had hissed the threat which was meant for her ears only.

'You bitch. I'll get you for this.'

White and shaking, she stood there as he passed.

CHAPTER ELEVEN

THE incident unnerved her. She thought about if for the rest of that evening, the image of Mr Banks and his pale eyes filled with hatred never leaving her.

But by the time the bright sun of an early December morning flooded in through the thin material of the curtains, the memory had receded. Time had trivialised the event, making his words seem futile and harmless, and she scolded herself for her fears and her overactive imagination.

She arrived on the ward to do an early round to find Mandy in a great state of excitement.

'Dr Fenton-Taylor's back!' she exclaimed. 'He's doing a ward round today!'

Louisa paid even stricter attention to all her patients and asked Mandy to check that all the temperature charts were up to date. She checked every new blood result, and saw to it that every drug chart was correctly signed and legible—she didn't want to let herself down in front of the big man!

She met him that afternoon, introduced rather abruptly by Adam. Dr Fenton-Taylor was a tall, imposing figure, dressed traditionally in the ubiquitous three-piece suit of the successful consultant. He shook hands with her and said he hoped she was enjoying the job.

'I'm sorry I've missed your first weeks,' he continued. 'But I'm sure my stand-in has taught you plenty!' He glanced at Adam, as did Louisa, but she noticed that he was steadfastly avoiding her gaze.

'Adam's been telling me how pleased he is with your work—praise indeed!'

Indeed, thought Louisa as she smiled back politely at her consultant. I'll bet he can't wait to see the back of me!

The ward round ran smoothly, and the whole team, bar Adam, congregated in the day-room afterwards for tea.

Louisa saw him stop the consultant by the door and say something quietly which made the latter chortle with laughter.

'Of course, dear boy! Back to your beloved test-tubes—I don't know how you've survived without them these past weeks!'

Louisa didn't know whether to be sorry or glad as she watched him go. She had wanted him to resume his research work so that she wouldn't see him so often, yet perversely she knew that she was going to miss him, even though they didn't speak much any more.

Why was life so complicated? she mused as she sipped the China tea which Mandy had provided.

She was the last to leave, hanging around listlessly as she helped to collect up the cups.

Mandy looked up from her tray, eyes shining behind the oversized glasses.

'Looking forward to the party, then?'

Louisa gazed at her blankly. 'Party? What party?'

'Tut, tut. The party next week—hasn't anyone told you about it? I'm surprised that Adam hasn't mentioned it.'

Adam had hardly spoken a word to her outside work since that wretched evening, she thought miserably as she shook her head.

Mandy beamed. 'Every year, Dr and Mrs Fenton-Taylor have a drinks party at their house—a great big affair. All his medical staff go, and the sisters and staff nurses from Dale and Belling. There's always wonderful eats and drinks—I can't wait! You can wear your new grey dress, can't you?'

'Yes,' she answered doubtfully, wondering if there was any way she could get out of it, dreading seeing Adam turning up with a girl, or having to endure Magda flirting with him all evening.

She couldn't get out of it, of course, not without offending her host. Because she was working with the team all day, she couldn't simply plead ill health, when they had all seen her tucking into a healthy lunch just a few hours earlier!

On the day of the party she arrived home to

find Adam in the kitchen, wearing only a white towelling robe, his hair still wet, his feet bare, making some coffee. Needless to say, he didn't bother to offer her any. She felt almost dizzy with embarrassment at the falsely intimate pose they struck, facing each other across the small room.

'Hi,' he said, as though the word and the small smile which accompanied it had cost him an effort. 'You'll want to use the bathroom, I suppose? Take your time—I've finished in there now.'

She nodded, catching the faint scent of shampoo and soap as he passed her, wishing that she could do or say something which would dispel the awful atmosphere between them.

She made herself some coffee and carried it through to the bedroom and drank it gazing glumly out at the dark turrets of the old hospital building before going through to run her bath.

She washed her hair in the basin and tied it up in a pink, fluffy towel, catching sight of her naked reflection as she bent to turn off the taps. She realised that the job suited her. She had always been slim, but the exercise gained from running around the wards had toned her up. Her tiny waist emphasised the curve of her hips and breasts and contrasted with her long legs, which had never looked so slender.

Blast Adam Forrester! she thought crossly as she lowered herself into the fragrant foam. He hadn't even offered to give her a lift to the

Fenton-Taylors'. Mandy was going straight there after a late duty, so she was forced to go on her own, armed with a crudely drawn map. Huw Lloyd was bringing his Welsh girlfriend, and Basil was taking his wife. Quite frankly, being forced to circulate with her colleagues was the last thing she felt like doing.

She applied her make-up—wearing more than her usual mascara, the gold-flecked eye shadow drawing attention to the large eyes of sapphire, and a faint slick of dark lipstick making her mouth provocatively wide. She dried her hair and brushed it vigorously, so that it gathered in a dark chestnut-coloured cloud around her face and shoulders. And lastly she climbed carefully into the grey wool dress, the dark sheer stockings and the high-heeled black patent shoes which made her look unusually tall. The soft cashmere moulded itself to every curve of her body, and over the bodice itself were sewn tiny beads which caught the light and sparkled like a scattering of stars.

She looked into the mirror and nodded. She knew she looked good and it gave her confidence. She was jolly well going to enjoy herself this evening—despite the unpredictable Adam. She found her car keys and snapped the catch of her black patent bag shut.

As she let herself out, she could hear music coming from his room. He seemed in no hurry to arrive either—at this rate she would get there before him. Outside it was a bitterly cold night.

The moon glimmered down from a clear sky and she was glad of her thick woollen jacket.

She walked quickly to her car which sat about five places away from Adam's Porsche. She had long since abandoned the idea of parking in his spot.

She climbed in and turned on the ignition, but as she did so she heard a well-known but dreaded whirring noise. She cursed silently and tried again, drumming her fingers impatiently on the steering wheel as she listened to the same sound.

Common sense told her that her repeated efforts to start the car were fruitless, but she continued nonetheless. Click, whirr. Click, whirr. Over and over again.

'Damn!' she shouted out loud, slamming the flat of her hand down against the steering wheel.

The rapping on her window made her jump and she looked up startled to see Adam leaning down outside.

He opened the driver's door. 'Having trouble?' he enquired mildly.

'Oh, no,' she replied caustically. 'This is my favourite way of spending a winter's evening!'

He sighed. 'Isn't this where we came in? Come on, leave it now—I'll give you a lift to the party.'

She couldn't think of anything worse than having to endure the knowledge that Adam had

been forced to accompany her. He could keep
his grudging charity!

'Oh, don't worry about me,' she announced
loftily. 'I'll manage to get her started—I always
do!'

'Louisa, you're just being stubborn. You
know as well as I do that your battery is as flat
as a pancake. Even if you were to put it on
charge immediately, it's not going to be ready
in time to get you there. Now, are you coming
or not?'

She felt like brazening it out, threatening to
get a cab or catch a bus, but there was a niggling
doubt at the back of her mind as to whether he
would actually tolerate such nonsense. From
the increasingly impatient expression on his
face, she could actually imagine him bundling
her into the car by force!

'Oh, very well,' she conceded sulkily, and
followed him over to his car. 'But I didn't even
want to go to the stupid party in the first place!'

'That makes two of us,' he said savagely. 'But
as courtesy demands that we go, you could try
to stop acting like a spoilt child and get in the
car!'

His anger and his disapproval of her came as
such a shock that she shut her mouth tight
automatically, afraid that if she moved a muscle
of her face she might begin to cry. She had
been wondering why he had chosen to avoid
her, and the reason now dawned on her. He
didn't have the slightest inclination to start a

relationship with her, in fact quite the opposite—he didn't seem to like her very much at all.

'Would you like to listen to some music?'

She shook her head silently, still afraid that she might cry. Damn him, and his mercurial nature! Did he think that he could mete out a sweetener to follow one of his insults and then everything would be all right?

The atmosphere in the car was unbearable. She was aware that he turned to look at her from time to time, and she set her face in a scowl, daring him to speak.

'Louisa——' he began finally, when at that moment there was a screech of brakes, and a flashing of light, followed by an almighty bang. Then silence.

'What in blazes. . .?' shouted Adam.

Louisa strained her eyes, animosity forgotten. 'It's an accident,' she told him in a shaking voice. 'Just up ahead, look!'

He jammed on his brakes immediately. Out of the gloom they could see two cars, one still standing, the other a mangled mess of metal which lay on its side.

Adam switched off the ignition and leapt out of the car. 'Stay there!' he ordered.

She watched him take a bag from the boot and go running towards the scene, before it occurred to her that she might be of assistance as well, and that he couldn't really stop her from following him—*she* was a doctor, too!

The high-heeled stilettos were stupidly impractical, she thought as she ran towards him.

He was kneeling down beside the passenger door of the overturned car, his face a picture of concern, and he was taking something from his bag.

When he caught sight of her he shouted 'For God's sake—be *careful*! The petrol tank could go up at any time. Check the other car and find out who's hurt. If there's a car phone then use it to call the ambulance and the fire brigade. If not then you'll have to flag down a car, but do it close by, where I can see you. When you've done that you can come back and help me.'

The shoes were too much impediment for what she had to do now, and she kicked them off and sped towards the other car. Inside were a man and a woman. The man was unconscious, his head resting against the steering wheel, and Louisa ran her fingers lightly over to the templar pulse at the side of his head—it was rapid, but strong. As she moved her fingers away, they came with the sticky warm texture of blood covering them. Without thinking, she wiped them down the front of her new dress.

The woman was conscious, but obviously in shock. She sat in the passenger seat, her eyes like saucers in a chalky face, little whimpering sounds coming from her throat.

'Have you a car phone?' asked Louisa.

The woman shook her head dumbly, tears beginning to well up in the corners of her eyes.

'Your husband is alive. You must both stay exactly as you are for the moment. I'm going to get someone to call an ambulance. Do you understand?'

The woman nodded and Louisa made her way gingerly to the side of the road. She realised that the dark coat would make her virtually indistinguishable from the blackness of the night, and so she took it off and threw it on to the damp grass of the verge, standing with her arms spread like a windmill by the edge of the road.

Fortunately, a car happened along almost immediately, and more importantly was driven by a sensible driver who was not inclined to interrogate or linger and who drove off at speed to contact the emergency services.

Louisa should have been frozen, but she knew that the adrenalin which was coursing around her body was protecting her from such normal reactions as cold and fear. She ran back over to Adam, and knelt down beside him.

'What's happening?' she whispered.

'Two teenagers. The driver's dead. The girl is bleeding badly—I think it's an artery in her leg. We're going to have to stop it. Can you hold the torch for me?'

She took the powerful light from him and positioned it as he gradually manoeuvred the door open. She could see the slight form of a very young girl, spiky hair now clotted with blood, a pair of dangling earrings looking incongruously huge.

'Can you take her pulse and still hold the torch steady?'

She complied. 'Feeble,' she told him. 'About a hundred and forty.'

She saw his eyes search the girl's lower limbs. 'Got it,' he muttered, and he applied a huge wad of gauze to the pumping vessel. The seconds ticked by, with Adam pushing all his weight on to the gauze to apply the direct pressure necessary to stem the flow, but she could see sweat beading his forehead, and lines of worry appear there.

'I don't like her pulse,' warned Louisa, feeling it become more fluttery.

'We're going to have to get her out of the car,' he decided. 'If she arrests in that position, we're done for. Can you do exactly as I say?'

Very carefully, they managed to lift the girl out of the crushed car between them, though Louisa never knew how they managed it. Her lightness made it easier, and when she was lying on the bank, Adam's job proved less difficult. But the girl was slipping, Louisa could feel it in her pulse, and she could see from the desperation on Adam's face that he felt it, too.

At the same moment that the wail of the siren pierced the still night air, and the ghostly blue light flickered into view, the girl's heart stopped beating.

'Brooke's airway by my feet,' shouted Adam.

Louisa delivered one short, sharp blow to the sternum and pulled the airway out of his bag. Tipping the head right back so that the neck was extended, she positioned it correctly and then began the life-saving technique. Pump, pump, pump, pump, puff. Four firm external massages applied to the heart, followed by one long blow of air into the lungs via the airway. Repeated until the heart restarted, or until the procedure had to be abandoned. . .

They could hear footsteps running frantically towards them now, and two ambulancemen appeared, their eyes swiftly taking in the scene before them. One of them recognised Adam.

'Get me an intravenous infusion set!' he shouted.

'Yes, Doctor!'

The pack arrived and one of the ambulancemen took over from Adam on the artery. Louisa continued with the resuscitation while Adam found a vein and rushed through almost half a litre of Haemaccel immediately and, miraculously, the girl's heart started beating again.

Things became blurred and confused then as more ambulances, police cars and the fire brigade arrived, with lights flashing and the sound of radios being switched on and off. Two doctors arrived from St Dunstan's and one of them helped Adam strap the girl's leg. Within minutes she was being rushed away in an ambulance, siren screaming hysterically.

Adam and Louisa stood there watching as it roared off, and he put his arm around her shoulder and squeezed it.

'You were great,' he said quietly. 'Really great.'

'So were you,' she responded, wishing that he'd move his arm, not trusting her reactions.

She didn't want to stay to see the rest—the gory aftermath of the boy's body being removed from the car. The experts were here now to deal with everything. Reaction was beginning to set in.

'I'd like to go now,' she muttered tiredly.

'We'd like a statement from you both, please,' said one of the policemen.

'Now?' Adam frowned.

'If you wouldn't mind, Doctor. It won't take very long.'

He shrugged. 'Fit enough?' he asked her and she nodded.

Adam slung his equipment back into his bag, and they hunted for Louisa's shoes, one of which was covered in mud and completely unwearable.

'Stupid-looking things,' he grumbled as he helped her back towards the car.

They travelled in a convoy to the police station, where they were given hot, sweet tea and had their statements taken. It was gone ten by the time they had made their way back to the Porsche.

Louisa had just rested her head back blissfully

when she sat bolt upright. 'The party!' she exclaimed.

Adam chuckled, his teeth looking almost as white as his ruffled shirt in the darkness. 'I think we could be excused, don't you? We're hardly dressed for it, are we?'

She glanced down at her blood-smeared dress, ripped stockings and shoeless feet, and began to smile as they gathered speed.

She yawned continually all the way back to the hospital, but his driving didn't seem at all affected. He was a cool cookie, she thought tiredly.

They parked the car back at the hospital, and made their way up to the flat. Louisa was longing for the reviving comfort of a long, hot bath. What a way to spend an evening off!

Adam unlocked the door and went directly to the phone to tell the Fenton-Taylors what had happened.

'Well, we're very sorry to have missed it, too—it was entirely unplanned, I can assure you, Dorothea!' He listened for a moment and then smiled. 'That would be delightful. I'll tell her.'

He replaced the receiver slowly and turned around. 'They want us to dine with them another evening.' As he spoke, his dinner jacket fell open, and under the harsh sitting-room light she caught sight of him properly for the first time since the accident. If she had thought that she was blood-covered, it was nothing in comparison to him. She gasped to see that the front of his shirt was literally covered in bright red arterial blood.

Instinctively she moved forward, her hand reaching out to touch him, but she saw him flinch and she dropped her hand, her hackles rising as she turned on him furiously. She wanted the truth out.

'What's the matter, Adam? Are you afraid to be in the same room as me? And don't try to deny you've been avoiding me, because I know damn well you have!' Her lip curled with scorn. 'Was it because you dared to confide in me that made you run away like a frightened rabbit? Or were you just concerned that, because we'd shared *one kiss*, I'd start behaving like some little medical groupie? No doubt you encountered enough of them on your stupid show!'

He was shaking his head. 'That's not true.'

She didn't heed his words—her attack was relentless. 'Did you think I'd start cooking you supper every night and leaping into your arms? Is that what you were afraid of? So sure of your own irresistibility?'

His face was very serious. 'You know that's not the reason why.'

She turned away from him, her voice trembling. 'I don't know anything. I thought. . . I thought we were friends.'

His voice sounded strained. 'I can't be your friend, Louisa.'

She didn't want to know any more, she was
sick and weary of the animosity. 'Go away.'

A muscle was working furiously in his cheek.
'I'm not going anywhere. You want the truth?
Well, then I'll give it to you. I can't be your
friend—how can I when every time I see you I
just want to take you in my arms and kiss every
last breath out of your body? Of course I've
been avoiding you, and do you know the reason
why?' He turned towards her helplessly. 'I can't
get you out of my mind, Louisa—don't you
know that? I wake, dream, eat, sleep, and all I
can think about is you, yes, you!'

Her eyes were like saucers. 'Because of one
kiss?' she asked incredulously.

He shook his head impatiently. 'Not because
of one kiss—that told me nothing more than I
already knew. That I want you. That I've
wanted you since the first time I ever saw you—
feisty and full of fire, so beautiful and challeng-
ing—getting out of that ridiculous car.'

He gave a bitter little laugh. 'I appalled
myself, really. I'd seen my wife that day, for the
first time in over a year—she thought it "civil-
ised" that we should have a farewell meal before
the divorce became finalised.' He gave another
hollow laugh.

'She was full of herself, of her affair. She
wanted to ridicule me, to taunt me, to make me
desire her again. But that had died—I could
never imagine desiring any woman ever again.
And then I saw you and I knew how fickle I

could be. It was a thunderbolt, and I wanted you. I've wanted you ever since.

'That first night when you clung to me, you were like a frightened little girl, so vulnerable that I wanted to protect you. The night I found you crying, I'd never felt such a heel in my life. That's when I thought we could be friends, but I was wrong.'

She could not believe what she was hearing. Her mind and body were locked in bitter combat. Oh, treacherous body, she thought desperately, as she felt the stirrings of need deep within her.

'Oh, Adam,' she cried softly. 'Why didn't you tell me?'

He was shaking his head with the desperation of someone trying to deny what they know to be the truth. 'Because there's no point!'

The flame within her was burning still more strongly. 'Why ever not?' she whispered.

'Because I can't offer you anything. I've just left one rotten marriage—I'm just not ready for another serious relationship at the moment.'

Images of her past flashed before her. This was a subject on which she was an expert—the so-called joys of commitment. She remembered Mike's barbs—that she had bartered sex for marriage—and what a marriage. Never again. She looked at the tall man who stood in front of her.

She liked him and respected him. She desired him with an intensity she had not thought it possible to feel. Some people might call that love. She recognised with a startling clarity that she would never meet a man like Adam Forrester again. In life you were sometimes fortunate to be given heaven-sent opportunities. This, she knew, was one of them. Was it so wrong to reach out for a little happiness, even if she knew it could not last?

He was shaking his head again. 'Louisa—it's not fair—I can't offer you anything,' he repeated.

Her lips curved into a knowing, confident smile and she knew he was lost.

'I'm not asking for anything. Only you.'

They were moving the few paces between them in tantalisingly slow motion, drawn each to the other as inexorably as iron filings to the magnet.

His long brown fingers incredulously stroked the softness of her face, brushing damp wisps of hair back, as if he couldn't see enough of her.

'Do you have any idea of how much I've longed for this moment?' he whispered, and she shook her head silently.

He stood and kissed her. Kissed her and kissed her until she thought she might faint. Then he drew away and she saw him looking down at their clothes, still covered with the mud and debris from the accident.

'We can't make love like this,' he whispered, and the anticipation of it sent her senses jangling.

With infinite care, as though she were the most precious package in the world, he slowly began to undress her. He slipped out of his own clothes and led her into the shower, his skin so very dark against her own, and turned the water jets on full power.

He washed every inch of her, and every inch he followed with the gentle touch of his lips, until she had reached a fever pitch of unbearable excitement. She clung to the strong firm contours of his wet shoulders, pressing her lips against the matted hair on his chest until he moaned aloud with delight.

She was scarcely aware of him carrying her through to his room, a room she had never before entered, or of him laying her down on the bed and taking her in his arms.

His lovemaking was all things—reverential, passionate, spiritual, explosive. She found herself in a strange new land, new sensations sweeping over her as she made her way towards some mysterious summit. And then she reached it, falling over with delight into a star-filled meadow and she called his name out loud, tears on his shoulder.

They lay in each other's arms, loud pulses gradually thudding back to normal, her eyes closed, longing to tell him the one thing which she knew would drive him away from her. That she loved him.

CHAPTER TWELVE

IT WAS strange, she reflected, how a single action could totally change your whole life, and yet ostensibly that life remained exactly the same. The French even had an expression for it—*plus ça change; plus c'est la même chose*—the more things change, the more they are the same.

How else could she explain the fact that her affair with Adam had just slotted into her life, as though it were the most perfectly natural thing in the world, as though all her life she had been waiting for him?

Sharing the same flat could have seemed claustrophobic, but it didn't. She spent every night in his bed and he taught her things about her body that she'd never dreamed of, or read about—not even in medical textbooks! She discovered, about twenty-four hours after she had calmly reassured him that she wanted nothing from him, that she had been foolishly wrong. She had met the man she could have happily spent the rest of her life with.

It made her realise how wrong she had been to marry Mike. *This* was how it should feel—this dizzy delirium which made her feel on a constant high. And she regularly blocked out the voice in her head which mocked her, asking her if she wasn't heading for the greatest hurt of her life.

Things were so easy with him—there was no conflict of interests as there had been with Mike. He liked taking her to bed, but he also liked studying, and he respected the fact that she did as well. He treated her as an equal—his job was neither no more nor less important than hers, and he wouldn't have dreamed of asking her to abandon writing notes in order to cook him supper, although ironically, for the first time in her life, she would have been willing to do so!

If only. . .

If only what? she asked herself sternly. If only he hadn't just come through a bad divorce? If only they could live together happily ever afterwards? But real life wasn't like that. He had been straight with her from the start, and she must respect that. She must just enjoy what they had now. Tomorrow would have to take care of itself.

By a tacit agreement, they did not make the affair public. Both knew the insatiable desire for gossip which existed in all small communities, and their lives touched in too many places—people would have a heyday knowing that they had started a relationship while sharing a flat. So Louisa continued to see Mandy occasionally, and to pay solo visits to the hospital games-room with some of the other house officers, though all the time she wanted to do nothing more than run back to the safe haven of their flat where none of the rest of the world could touch them. Safe in his arms, safe beneath the fervent kisses he bestowed on her.

It was almost perfect. Almost. Because she knew that they were both holding back. There could not be the same emotional investment in a relationship which was never going to be serious.

Since the night he had confessed his feelings to her, he had never mentioned his wife to her again, and she was glad. Perhaps because of his steadfast refusal to mention the future, she offered him nothing of her past, and he never asked. The last thing she wanted to do in the time they had together was to have to relate the whole story of her doomed marriage to Mike.

He had an old-fashioned charm about him, and he seemed to think that she expected to go out to expensive places. The first time he took her out to dinner, they drove to a small olde worlde restaurant on the outskirts of Dunchester. It looked ravishing, with its dark oak beams, low ceilings, and snowy linen adorned with small vases of fragrant pinks.

But it had been impossibly formal, with waiters converging on them with *crudités* and damask napkins the size of tablecloths almost before they had even had a chance to take their seats. Each time one of them opened their mouth to speak, another waiter would pour more wine, drop a newly warmed bread roll into the basket, or smarmingly ask if 'everything is all right, sir?'

At last she put her knife and fork down on the plate and burst out laughing. 'Just what are we doing here, Adam?'

He looked mildly surprised raising his eyebrows. 'I thought all young women liked to be taken to places like this?'

He had a very stereotyped view of women, she mused. He had been shocked when she had admitted that she didn't really like his Porsche, and she suspected that material wealth had been very important to his wife.

'Not this one,' she answered firmly. 'This one prefers an omelette on the kitchen table, courtesy Adam Forrester!'

'And what would you like to follow?' he murmured.

She had learnt to play the coquette to these remarks.

'What would you suggest?' she whispered across to him.

They left the meal mid-course, much to the waiters' chagrin, and it took some convincing for Adam to reassure them that there had been nothing wrong with the meal. How could they tell them that they simply couldn't wait to be alone again? That they couldn't keep their hands off each other?

He chased her across the car park, catching her as she reached the car, pressing her against it and kissing her hungrily. And when he finally raised his head, he looked at her for a long moment with a face full of some indescribable emotion, to which tenderness contributed, that she had to hurriedly turn her head away, for fear that he should see how much she needed him.

She was half ashamed that she was allowing him to dictate all the terms of the relationship, allowing herself to settle for something less than she wanted. But what was her alternative? She loved him too much to ever give him up voluntarily.

At least, because he had resumed his research, they met infrequently at work, for she was convinced that her body language was shrieking out loudly her feelings for him, whenever he was around.

A letter was handed in to the hospital administrator, addressed to Dr and Mrs Forrester, and according to Adam Mrs Jefferson's face had been a picture when she had handed it over! It was from the young girl who had been involved in the road traffic accident, thanking them for all they had done for her. She had sustained a fractured clavicle, and tibia, and would only have to spend a few short weeks in hospital.

'The ambulancemen told my mum what you did for me. They said that if you and Mrs Forrester hadn't come along when you did, that I would not be alive today. I owe you my life, and for that I am forever in your debt.'

Louisa had tears in her eyes when Adam

handed it to her, happy beyond belief that the young girl had lived, but she felt ridiculously weepy that she had been mistaken for his wife. It was what she would have wished for more than anything else.

She realised with a start that there was only a short time until Christmas, when Adam returned home one day waving the rota.

'We're on call,' he announced.

She looked up frowning, her mind still on cardiomyopathy.

'When?'

He came over to her and grinned, kissing the top of her head.

'Why, Christmas of course, my little blue-stocking! Don't you ever have anything on your mind but work?'

She put her pen down and stretched languor-ously, her arms above her head, knowing that he was watching her every movement. 'Come to bed and I'll show you.'

She went as if to pass him, but he caught her in his arms. 'Louisa, sweetest—your capacity for enjoyment never ceases to amaze me, and you look as though butter wouldn't melt in that beautiful mouth!' His lips drowned her laughter.

Skin against skin. Heartbeats gradually slowing. She opened her eyes to find him stroking strands of hair away from her face. He picked up her hand and began to kiss her fingers slowly, one by one.

'That's lovely,' she said sleepily.

'So are you.' There was a pause. 'This means we'll be able to spend Christmas together.'

'Oh, Adam!' Her arms flew round his neck.

'Do I take it you're for the idea?' he chuckled. 'Even if it means dry turkey in the canteen?'

'Not on your life! I'll cook us Christmas lunch here.'

She felt as though the gods had given her a very special gift, and she vowed very hard not to offend them in any way, for fear they would take it away from her. She wanted to make this the best Christmas ever.

Adam was due to go and visit his cousins in Sussex the weekend before Christmas. Cornwall was too far to go for just a weekend and so she had telephoned Aunt Beatrice to tell her that she would take a week's holiday towards the end of her job.

Like her, Adam had no parents—his had both died within the year just after he had started medical school and it was another reason why she wanted to make this Christmas happy. They would see in a bright New Year together—and who knew what the year ahead would bring?

She said goodbye to him at the door of the flat on the Saturday morning, and he held her very tightly in his arms, his head bowed on to her shoulder.

'I'm going to miss you, Lulu,' he said, in a gruff voice.

'I'm going to miss you, too,' she gulped.

After he had gone, she drove the car into town, parking in the multi-storey car park in the precinct. She had been deliberating all week what to cook on Christmas Day, and now the menu was complete, bearing in mind that they might get called to the wards at any time, and that it would be unfair on the patients to eat a lot of garlic!

There were to be wedges of golden sweet melon to start, with slivers of Parma ham. For the main course—duck with a black cherry sauce, dauphine potatoes and mange-tout—all things which would keep—with Christmas pudding and brandy butter to finish.

She glanced down at the shopping list. Some of these things she could buy today, but she would have to come to town again later in the week.

As she locked the car, she noticed a movement out of the corner of her eye, but when she looked towards the spot it was completely empty. The car park was deserted and she shivered a little. Oh, stop being so daft, she remonstrated with herself—you've been watching far too many American detective shows!

She went to McCormack's—the large Irish-owned department store which stocked just about everything. She bought a dark brown cashmere shawl for Aunt Beatrice—just the job for those freezing Cornish winters! For Mandy she purchased a cookery book which she knew she wanted.

Choosing something for Adam proved much more difficult. She wanted to buy him hundreds of presents, but she didn't want to overdo it. Bother convention, she thought crossly, as she gazed longingly at a V-necked sweater in the softest lambswool which would have set his dark hair and blue eyes off perfectly. In the end she bought him nothing, vowing to think about it during the week and to buy something when she came back for more ingredients for their Christmas lunch.

She stopped for a salad and a coffee in the bright, airy rooftop restaurant, and was unable to resist buying liqueur chocolates and pistachio nuts in the luxury food hall. It was almost four-fifteen by the time she walked back to the car park, weighed down by all her packages. But her stupid fear of being watched persisted, and several times she spun round nervously to see some innocent customer looking rather taken aback by her close scrutiny.

In the dark car park she fumbled with her keys, finally locking herself in her car with relief, to discover that she was shaking.

But back in the flat she felt safe once more, and she unpacked her shopping, singing happily underneath her breath. She found herself soppily wanting to iron two of Adam's shirts, but didn't dare. It must be love—she hated ironing!

It was the first night that they had spent apart, and although she missed him, she nevertheless enjoyed the luxury of a long bath, and supper on a tray in front of the television. At eight o'clock, she sat wondering what he was doing now. He hadn't told her a great deal about his cousin, but she knew that he was married with a small child, and that they lived in a big old house in the middle of some glorious Sussex countryside.

As if in answer to her thoughts, the phone began ringing and she picked up the receiver eagerly.

'Hello?'

There was a pause. 'Hello, Lulu.'

It was as if she hadn't heard him speak for weeks. 'Adam! How lovely to hear from you. Are you having a nice time?'

'I am. It would be even better if you were here with me.'

Calm down, she told herself, her pulse rate soaring at his words. It wasn't the best of connections—it sounded as if someone was rustling a plastic bag somewhere on the line, and she could hear distant voices, too. 'It sounds very lively there.'

He laughed. 'They've arranged a dinner party in my honour.'

She couldn't help herself. 'Oh?' she enquired sulkily.

'Why, Lu,' he teased her, 'I do believe you might be jealous!' A pause. 'You've no reason to be—no one here could hold a candle to you.'

Her heart had resumed its crazy erratic dance. 'I should hope not!'

'I'd better not stay—they're threatening to start without me. Louisa. . .' He cleared his throat, and his voice was so quiet that she could hardly hear him. 'I want to talk to you when I get back. I should be with you by early evening. All right?'

'Yes.' She felt suddenly shy, suddenly apprehensive.

'Bye then.'

'Bye.'

She replaced the receiver thoughtfully. What did he want to talk to her about? Was he afraid that things were becoming too serious?

She walked through to the kitchen to wash up, deciding that it would only give her a sleepless night if she started surmising about what he might, or might not say.

But despite all her good resolutions, she slept fitfully and the feeling of unease which had haunted her all day remained. She dreamt strange, formless dreams causing her to wake in the impenetrable blackness of the night, disorientated and frightened, and the next morning she awoke with an unaccustomed splitting headache. She drank some strong coffee, and even took two aspirins, but the dull aching behind her temples just would not go away.

She was jittery and on edge, missing Adam, not knowing what to do with herself. She tried reading a textbook, but had to abandon it. She picked up a novel, but it was no use—she was not in the mood for the written word. Eventually she put on her windcheater, some sturdy shoes and jeans and tied her hair back. She would go for a long walk—*that* should get rid of her headache!

She left the hospital on foot, taking only about twenty minutes to cover the distance to the pretty woods Mandy had told her about. The air was crisp and clear, the sky the brilliant forget-me-not blue of a perfect December day. Scarlet berries glistened on the lush foliage of the holly, and she sniffed the air appreciatively. If only Adam were here to share it with her.

Once or twice she found herself looking over her shoulder anxiously, again with that feeling that she was not alone. Once she heard the sound of a twig cracking and it unnerved her. It had probably only been the sound of some small animal, but it had been enough to destroy her pleasure in the walk. She hurried home, almost breaking into a run as she left the woods, disproportionately pleased to see the dark outline of the hospital loom up before her.

Roll on this evening, she thought as she rode up to the fifth floor in the lift. She couldn't wait to see him again. Maybe then she would be able to laugh about her stupid fears.

She let herself into the flat, slamming the

front door behind her and she went immediately into the sitting-room, turning on the electric fire to warm the room up.

The sound of the doorbell shattered her solitude, sounding unnaturally loud, and she jumped. She wasn't expecting anyone.

Oh, pull yourself together, she thought grimly. You've never been a shrinking violet before! Nevertheless, she made sure that the chain was on the door before she opened it.

She did not know who she had been expecting, but certainly not the sturdy figure who stood before her now. Her mouth fell open in surprise. What on earth was he doing here?

'Well? Aren't you going to invite me in?'

She gulped. It seemed she had no choice.

'Hello, Mike,' she said quietly.

CHAPTER THIRTEEN

SHE fumbled with the chain to unlock the door, and he stepped inside, standing in front of her with a grin on his face. Her husband. The man she had married. Somehow the shock of seeing him again overcame her, and she felt a wave of dizziness sweep over her.

'You'd better come in,' she muttered, leading the way into the small sitting-room—the room which only a few minutes ago had seemed chilly, now feeling overbearingly, cloyingly hot from the fire.

He stood with his back to the fireplace, and she looked at him properly for the first time in years.

He stood at just a head taller than her, powerfully built, with the broad shoulders of a natural rugby player, but she noticed a slight paunch where a once flat stomach had been. It shocked her to think that one day Mike might run to fat. His fair hair gleamed in the same irrepressible waves that she remembered, but his eyes were bloodshot, and there were faint lines of dissipation beginning to show on his skin. She realised with a pang that the conquering sporting hero had been lost forever, swallowed up by intemperate living, no doubt, and she was filled with a great sadness for what might have been. She had, after all, loved him once, or had thought that she loved him—and he would always be a part of her past, and her youth.

She saw that he had been observing her too, and was staring at her now in that same confidently casual manner he'd always had.

'Wow!' he said softly. 'You're looking good.'

A thought occurred to her. 'Have you been following me?' she demanded crossly, and the instant she saw his grin she knew that her guess had been correct.

'I had to choose my moment,' he protested, in his little-boy-lost voice, shrugging his shoulders. 'Check that I wasn't stepping on anybody's toes.'

'I've been edgy all weekend,' she complained. 'Why are you here? What do you want?'

He gave an expression of mock dismay. 'What a way to talk to your ex-husband!' His eyes were taking in everything. 'How does it feel? Being a free woman again, I mean?' He glanced around the room. 'Although, if I'm not mistaken, I can see all the signs of masculine occupation.' He raised his eyebrows questioningly. 'But you can tell me all about it over a drink, can't you, Louisa?'

She frowned. 'For God's sake, Mike—it's only eleven o'clock in the morning.'

'Ever the prude, my darling, aren't you? But you don't have the right to nag me any more, you know! Just pour me out a large whisky, there's a good girl!'

She hesitated for a moment, then walked over to the array of bottles on the sideboard. She couldn't really boot him out the moment he'd arrived, could she? Her hand shook slightly as she tipped a measure of the spirit into the glass. It was Adam's whisky, but he rarely touched it.

'Water?'

'Bad memory. I'll take it straight, please.'

She was tempted to remind him that as students they hadn't been able to afford such luxuries as bottles of whisky, but what was the point? He was obviously getting her confused with someone else.

She watched as he downed the drink in one and held out his glass for a refill. That one movement brought home to her how miserably they had lived together as man and wife.

She poured him another drink. 'What are you doing here?' she asked again, not unpleasantly.

He shrugged. 'I've been for a job interview in Sheffield. I knew you were working here— thought I'd call in and see you. For old times' sake.'

It was strange to be sitting in Adam's flat, making polite conversation with the man to whom she had once been married. She noticed that his hand trembled very slightly as he laid the glass down.

'How are you doing, Louisa? Decided on your speciality yet?'

She shook her head. 'Not really—I thought I had, but now I don't know. It's early days yet. How about you?'

He swallowed the last of his drink with a grimace. 'Oh, I was quite set on surgery, until I fell out with my last boss. Don't know what I'm going to do next. I can't really see me switching to general practice, and that's so damned competitive now. Finding a job is getting harder and harder these days.'

He's drinking far too much, she thought, and already he had the air of someone who would only ever be second best. Extraordinarily, she felt sorry for him.

'And Kirsty?' she enquired gently. 'How is she?' Strange how she could now calmly say the name of the girl he'd been with that day.

'Kirsty?' he laughed. 'She didn't last long.' He looked up at her, and the blood-shot eyes were serious for a moment. 'You were a very hard act to follow, you know.' He glanced around the room again, his gaze coming to rest on the dark blue silk tie which Adam had left on the table. 'But you've found someone else?'

'Yes, I have.'

'And you're happy?' He gave a click of annoyance. 'That's a pretty dumb question, isn't it? You look wonderful. You must be happy.'

'Very happy.' But insecure, she thought. How surprised he would be if he knew of the no-strings basis of her relationship with Adam.

He stood up suddenly. 'I shouldn't have

come. It was silly, really. I just wanted you to know. . .' He shook his head, as though he'd changed his mind. 'It doesn't matter. I'm sorry things went sour between us.'

She too stood up. 'I'm sorry, too. We were both too young. I've often felt that I forced you into it, that if it hadn't been for my stupid old-fashioned attitude you wouldn't have had to marry me.'

His voice was sad. 'No one made me do it, Louisa. I'd have wanted to marry you anyway. It was the best thing I ever did in my whole life, only I was too foolish to see it at the time. And I blew it.'

She knew what he was saying, but it was too late for them now. And quite suddenly she made her mind up that she would tell Adam about Mike. She had been wrong—you couldn't just live for the moment, because the present was made up of little bits of the past. She was who she was because of all the things that had happened in her life before.

They stood in the hallway and he held his hand out to her.

'Goodbye, Louisa. All the best.'

The silly little words and phrases that you used in times of great emotion, she thought, as she took his outstretched hand and grasped it warmly.

His eyes met hers, suddenly hopeful. 'How about a kiss? Just for old times' sake?'

'What good would that do?' she asked gently.

'A hug then.' He put his arms around her shoulders and held her very close. She felt almost maternal as she hugged him back.

She heard it before he did. The sound of a key in the lock, a swishing sound as the door was pushed open. They fell apart guiltily, like secret lovers—and then she saw his face, the smile of welcome turning into an expression of disbelief.

Mike grinned at Adam and, as a brief look of disgust crossed the latter's face, she knew that he had smelt the alcohol.

'Whoops! Bad timing! I was just going, actually.'

Adam's voice was wintry. 'Aren't you going to introduce us, Louisa?'

Her normal tone seemed to have risen by a couple of octaves. 'Adam Forrester—Michael Gray.'

Adam ignored Mike's hand. A frown creased his forehead. 'Gray?'

Her voice came out as a croak. 'Mike is. . .We were once married,' she finished lamely.

'I see.' The blue eyes were like chips of ice.

Mike was looking quickly from one to the other. 'I think I'd better go. Thanks for the drink.'

She didn't really notice him leaving, her eyes were watching Adam.

'It isn't how it must seem.'

She had never seen him look so supercilious. 'Isn't it? Perhaps you'd care to explain?'

She could have borne his anger or his rage,

welcomed it almost, but not this cold, hard, indifferent face.

'He was just passing through—he'd been for a job interview in Sheffield, and decided to call in and see me. I haven't seen him in years— we've been divorced a long time now.'

'And you expect me to believe that?'

She couldn't believe this was happening. Not to them. 'Of course I do! It's the truth.'

He turned away from her. 'And you say that's all that went on?'

A slow flame of anger began to burn. 'Just what do you think went on, Adam? Tell me that.'

'What am I supposed to think?' he demanded, fury beginning to break through the mask of icy contempt. 'I go away for a night and come back—early, I might add—to find you in the arms of some drunken bum who, you charmingly inform me, is your ex-husband. I didn't even know you'd been married—that was one little fact you kept carefully hidden from me, wasn't it? I wonder what else you haven't told me?'

'Oh, for goodness' sake,' she exploded. 'Have you stopped to ask yourself *why* I didn't mention him? Could it have something to do with the fact that you told me there was no future for us? You made all the rules, Adam. And anyway, why should I tell you? You didn't want to know anything about me, did you? You wanted the involvement kept to a minimum.

'And you still haven't answered my question. Do you imagine for one moment that I sneaked him in here the moment you went away? Do you think we've been making love all night in your flat? Is that the kind of behaviour you think I'm capable of? I'm not Clara, you know—and the sooner you stop using her as a touchstone, then the happier you'll be.'

He stared out of the window. 'You lied to me.'

'I did *not* lie to you.' Had she ever felt she really knew this cold-eyed man?

'It was a lie by omission.'

'Oh, for God's sake! This isn't a court of law— this is real life.' She laughed. 'But all this probably comes as a relief to you, doesn't it? You've had your fun and now I've given you the easy way out. Now you can go back to your safe little non-trusting world—where no one gets hurt, but no one lives either!

'You can't go through life by protecting yourself against possible involvement. OK—you had a bad experience—so did I. But that doesn't mean that I'm not prepared to take another chance. That's what life is all about!'

'I think you've said enough.' She could hear the barely contained fury in his voice.

'Too right, I have.' Afraid of the tears which were imminent, she half ran, half stumbled to her room. If he had come after her then, taken her in his arms, it could have all been all right.

But he didn't. She didn't need to hear the

door slamming to know that he had gone. The tearing pain in her heart was enough to tell her that too much had been said. She knew with a bitter certainty that he was gone from her forever.

CHAPTER FOURTEEN

TEARS poured down her cheeks as she threw herself on to the bed, her anger evaporating by the moment. Why, why, why had she turned on him?

Yes, he had jumped to conclusions, but could she really blame him? How would *she* have felt if she had returned from a night away to find him hugging his ex-wife? Particularly if she hadn't known that such a person existed?

He had done nothing wrong to her—he had been honest right from the start. If you couldn't stand the heat. . .

She lay staring up at the ceiling, her tears gradually drying, thinking of how differently she might have handled things. Why hadn't she told him about Mike? Because she had been too frightened. Too frightened to jeopardise the already shaky foundations of their relationship. But ironically she had now destroyed everything. The tight, cold look on his face had told her that it was too late to make amends—he would never trust her again.

And it was time to start being realistic. The relationship had been doomed right from the beginning, when he had told her that he 'couldn't offer her anything'. A love affair was like a flower—it needed not only care and attention, but room to grow and to flourish—no wonder that theirs had withered at the very first hurdle. What hope was there if the subject of the future was taboo, and if any mention of the past was scrupulously avoided?

She had thought that she was mature and sophisticated enough by now to handle a light-hearted fling—how stupid and naïve she had been. At heart she was still the vulnerable little girl she had always been, or else why would she be lying here, clutching on to her pillow as tightly as if it had been Adam Forrester himself?

It was a cruel fate that had brought Mike back into her life at so inopportune a moment. She sat up and looked round the sparsely furnished room. At least in a way, some good had come out of the whole business—the fact that now they had said their goodbyes amicably. She would waste no more time hating him, or blaming herself for the hastily conceived marriage. The past was dead and buried; she must look to the future now.

A small sob erupted from somewhere at the back of her throat for a future that looked as bleak and as barren as a desert landscape without Adam. The man she loved body, mind and soul. The man who satisifed every aspect of her complex personality—intellectual and physical. Could anyone ever match up to him? She scrubbed at her eyelids with the back of her fist. A stupid question.

Her mouth felt dry and her stomach empty. Her watch told her that it was now almost five o'clock and that she really ought to eat something. She got up from the bed shakily and glanced into the mirror. What a wreck she looked with white skin and red-rimmed eyes.

Automatically she reached for the hairbrush, untied the ribbon and brushed her hair until it looked presentable again. She washed her face and hands in cold water and felt better for having done so, then made herself some coffee.

She drank it in the kitchen, looking at the tiny room which in the space of a few short weeks had seemed like the best home she had ever had. But now he had gone it had reverted to being an anonymous little hospital flat, devoid of all life and colour.

She sat there for almost an hour, drinking sip after sip of coffee which she did not even taste, putting her cup down finally to admit to herself that he was not coming back, certainly not today. There would be no more scenes or recriminations, no chance of reconciliation—and had she really expected that there would be? Had she forgotten the way he had looked at her the moment before he had stormed out of the flat, and out of her life? All the affection had been gone from the icy blue eyes which had studied her with such distaste.

And then the lonely silence was broken by the ringing of the telephone, and she almost ran to pick it up.

'Hello?' she said breathlessly, then could have wept with disappointment when she heard the voice of the switchboard operator.

'Dr Gray?'

'Speaking.' She scarcely recognised the flat tone as her own.

'Casualty have just rung up to say that there's a letter for you there, and they wondered if you'd like to collect it.'

Her heart started thumping with renewed hope. 'A letter? For me? Do you know who from?'

The voice sounded mildly surprised. 'No, of course I don't, Doctor. I'm just passing on the message. They've left it in Sister's office.'

'Right, thank you. I'll pick it up right away. Thanks very much.'

Calm down. Calm down, she told herself as she hurried out. It may not be from him.

But who else would it be from? Anyone else would have sent the note to her flat. Unless that someone was Adam—couldn't face her at the moment, wanted to write it all down instead. Hadn't he once told her that he'd been far more successful behind the protective barrier of the written word than he had with the spoken one?

Her head was telling her that she shouldn't be behaving like this, that even if he had written to her he might simply be telling her that the relationship was at an end. But her heart, crazy love-torn heart, was filled with an irrational hope that speeded her footsteps towards the

Casualty Department. What they had had was far too good to end so abruptly. Another chance. That was all they needed.

The Casualty Office was empty save for Alistair McDavid, the young Scottish doctor who had started there recently, and he looked at her blankly when she asked him for an envelope addressed to her. They hunted around for a bit, and he eventually found it in the top drawer of Sister's desk, where she had obviously placed it for safekeeping.

'Here it is,' he said eventually, straightening up and handing it to her.

'Thanks.' She could see immediately that it was not from Adam—there was nothing of his loose, flowing style in the ill-formed and badly written letters of 'Dr Grey' which were inscribed on the front.

'They've spelt your name wrong,' commented Alistair as he watched her rip it open. 'Who's it from?'

She took out the small, cheap Christmas card, read the uniform greeting inside, and the childish scrawl underneath. 'From a friend.'

There was something sinister in the anonymous greeting, and she shivered, suddenly frightened.

'Who's it from?' repeated Alistair, watching her closely.

'I've no idea,' she replied, wishing that she could dispel the faint cloud of fear which hung over her.

She started to leave, but he stopped her.

'Listen, Louisa,' he said in his soft Scottish burr. 'Are you sure you're all right?'

She smiled, wondering if he'd noted her swollen eyes. 'Of course I'm all right. Goodnight, Alistair.'

'Goodnight.' Then, almost as an afterthought, he called after her. 'Happy Christmas!'

'Happy Christmas!' Some hopes of that, she thought as she left the office, walking slowly back along the corridor and a noise she heard behind her made her jump. She whirled round. Nothing. She was getting really neurotic, she decided. It had been bad enough yesterday, but at least then there had been a reason for her nerves, because Mike *had* been following her. But now Mike had gone. Was she really suggesting that someone else was watching her? The idea was so far-fetched as to be almost laughable.

So that she hardly heard the whisper of a step behind her, hardly realised that someone was right on her heels. Too late, she spun round to confront the childish face, contorted with a primitive rage which was terrifying in its intensity.

And with it came an almighty whoop—a kind of high, disconnected scream which became a shout, and a word wailed which sounded like gibberish, but which gradually formed itself into a distinguishable sound.

A word repeated again and again, in increasing volume as a large tattooed arm was flung around her neck. She saw Alistair McDavid's horrified face at the other end of the corridor just before she was dragged backwards into the empty room.

CHAPTER FIFTEEN

'Bitch,' he said, but softly this time. The vacant, rather stupid blue eyes were fixed on her face.

'You bitch,' he said again.

She cleared her throat, making a noise which sounded nervous, which surprised her, because she felt oddly detached as she stared at the pale, piggy face. But at least he had released her.

'Hello, Mr Banks. It *is* Mr Banks, isn't it?' she asked politely in a conversational tone. She might have been asking him to pass her the marmalade.

She thought at first that he hadn't heard her, for he continued to stare at her balefully.

'Mr Banks?' she prompted.

'You bitch.' The reply was hissed back, spat at her, words dripping vitriol. 'They've taken me kid away. They've taken me kid away and it's all thanks to you. What kind of bloody Christmas d'you think we're going to have without my boy? What do you think you've done to us? You bloody bitch.'

Her mouth dried with fear as she looked closely at him.

The pale eyes blazed in a kind of hopeless

rage. The mind of a boy trapped in the body of a man. Trapped. As trapped as she was.

She tried to remember back to her laughably brief spell of psychiatry, but she had worked on the firm which had dealt with phobias and obsessions—she had not come into contact with any violence, certainly not any violence directed at herself. What on earth should she do next?

The doorhandle was being rattled furiously. She heard Alistair's voice.

'Louisa? What's going on? Louisa!'

Mr Banks drew his hand swiftly across his neck in a gesture of command. 'Shut it,' he hissed.

She didn't dare do anything but comply. There was no more rattling. She heard Alistair's footsteps running down the corridor. For a split second she thought longingly of the man she loved, wished she were far away in his arms. Somewhere far away from this sordid and terrifying scene. And then she remembered. It was finished between them. She would gain no solace in Adam's arms any more, and in a way, that was far worse than the predicament she was in now.

She turned desperately towards the giant of a man who had imprisoned her. 'It isn't going to do you any good keeping me here, Mr Banks— it's only going to make matters worse.'

'Worse?' Scorn poured from his voice. 'You don't know nothing, do you? How could my life get any worse than it is now?'

'You must understand. I wanted to help Bobby—and to help you, too——'

'Help?' he interrupted. 'Is that what you think taking me kid away did? Do you think it helped the missus, with him going into care all over Christmas?'

'Yes, I do.' Her voice rose in her effort to try to make him understand. 'Tell me honestly, Mr Banks—*did* you ever hurt Bobby?'

She could hear the toot of a train in the distance. She watched the second hand of the clock on the wall as it performed its monotonous circular dance. Had he even heard the question she'd asked him?

'Did you?' she repeated quietly.

He gave a shuddering kind of sigh. 'Yes.'

She didn't for a moment underestimate the danger of her situation, but she closed her eyes tightly with relief for a brief second. The fear lifted, just a little. Acceptance of a problem was the first step to curing it and she looked at her assailant with renewed hope.

'Things are bad for you just now—and you were taking it out on your son. It happens. Bobby's removal need only be temporary—it will take the heat out of the situation—give you the chance to have counselling, to make you realise *how* the problem arises, and to teach you how to avoid striking out. Do you understand what I'm saying?'

She held her breath as the pale eyes stared at her, as if beginning to comprehend, for the first time, just what she was saying to him. The large, putty-like face crumpled and she watched as he dropped to his haunches, burying his head in his hands and rocking to and fro in a foetal position.

She walked over to him, watching as silent sobs racked his large frame.

'It's all right, Mr Banks. Everything is going to be all right.'

She rested her hand on his shoulder—a gesture of comfort from doctor to patient. She could have rushed to unlock the door, but she knew that she was quite safe. Now.

There were new sounds outside the door. More footsteps and voices. Lots of them.

'Open up! It's the police.'

She looked down at the slumped, broken figure and started for the door in a strange, dreamlike trance, when she heard a voice she knew so well, but a voice tainted by some unfamiliar emotion.

'Louisa! For God's sake, Louisa—speak to me.'

There was an almighty thump as something, or somebody was hurled against the door, and then protesting voices. She turned the key in the lock and pulled the door open to find Adam, his face a grey colour, his arms held firmly by two policemen.

She wasn't really aware of the small crowd— the policemen who tumbled into the office behind her, the frantic expressions on the faces of the onlooking nurses and doctors—she simply saw the anguished expression in the eyes of a man who had gazed over the edge of an abyss. Had she really made him feel so much pain?

'Lulu, are you OK?' he whispered, and silently she nodded.

And then somehow she was in his arms, the bitter words and angry scene forgotten as she nestled in the safe haven of his tight embrace, slowly coming back to life. He was holding her so close and muttering distractedly into her neck.

'Darling, darling Lu—I'm so sorry. I love you so much. I'll never let you go again. Can you ever forgive me? Louisa—my darling.'

Love? Had she heard him properly? Had he said he loved her?

And then, to her consternation, there came an enormous cheer and sounds of clapping and they both looked up to find the laughing faces of their colleagues applauding them.

Sister Hindmarsh cleared her throat. 'If you're about to propose marriage, Dr Forrester, then might I suggest you choose somewhere a little more private?'

Louisa buried her head against his chest, her cheeks scarlet, mortified with embarrassment. Well, that would have put the kibosh on things. He might have mentioned love, but he would run a mile from the thought of remarriage, and he certainly wouldn't thank Sister for daring to bring the subject up in front of the assembled masses.

'Come on, Lu. I'm taking you home.' To her surprise, he didn't sound a bit cross.

Still with his arm firmly around her shoulders, he led her through their now dispersing but still grinning colleagues, out of the building and into the fresh air outside.

The sky was a deep, clear indigo and their breath left smoky swirls all around them. She spared a thought for Mr Banks—she was not going to press any charges against him—there was no anger in her heart towards him, only a forlorn hope that his life might improve.

Inside the flat she trembled as he took her in his arms, kissed her eyelids, her cheeks, and her lips—tiny butterfly kisses that obliterated all feeling except desire.

'I want to take you to bed and make love to you for the rest of the day,' he said huskily. 'But there are a lot of things we have to get sorted out before we do that. Aren't there?'

'I should have told you that I'd been married,' she began, but he interrupted her with a finger placed on her lips.

'Yes, you should. And if I hadn't been so didactic with you from the start, then you might not have been too frightened to tell me.'

'I wasn't frightened,' she protested.

'No?' His eyes glinted.

'Well, a bit,' she admitted. 'I didn't want to rock the boat. I was happy being with you and I wanted things to stay just as they were. I realise now that things never remain static.'

'No, they don't.' His voice was very serious. 'And what's more, I've realised we wouldn't want them to, either. I seem to have done a lot of thinking since I stormed out of the flat.

'Life is about growth—and change. Sometimes we welcome the change, and sometimes we fight it. I've been fighting my feelings for you every inch of the way. I'm through with fighting it any more.' He sat down on the battered old sofa and pulled her on to his lap. 'And I owe you a big apology.'

She sighed and rested her head on the strong line of his shoulder. She was beginning to feel more secure by the second. 'No, you don't,' she murmured. 'You don't have to say anything.'

'Oh, but I do. Accusing you of fooling around while I was away was a cheap thing to do, because while I haven't known you that long— I feel that I know you better than anyone else in the whole world. And you're loyal and loving— so very loving, my darling girl.

'I spent the weekend at my cousin's missing you in a way I'd never experienced before. I couldn't wait to get back to you, to tell you how I felt. I'm afraid that when I saw you. . . I just——'

'Shh. It doesn't matter. I would probably have done the same. It was wrong of me to take you to task.'

'On the contrary, it was good for me. I need a

woman like you, Lulu. Someone warm, someone strong.'

'Strong? Me?'

'Yes, you. You're everything I've ever wanted in a woman—you're funny, and sexy and clever. And very beautiful. But. . .' He hesitated and lifted her chin.

Now comes the pay-off, she thought. She met his gaze unwaveringly. He thought that she was strong, well then, she would be strong. 'But?'

'I was wrong when I said I wanted no commitment. With you I want everything. All or nothing. Look,' his face as he spoke had the vulnerable expression on it she'd seen once before. 'I know it's far too soon, and I know we've both had bad experiences—but. . .Would you marry me?'

She almost fell off his lap. 'Marry you?'

Now he was animated. 'I know you've got your career to think about, I know that and I'll support you every inch of the way, but oh, Louisa—I love you so much and I want you to be my wife, it's as simple as that.'

She gave a low, gurgling laugh of pleasure. 'Oh, Adam. Of course I'll marry you. I think I've loved you almost from the first moment I met you.'

'And that—that maniac didn't lay a finger on you?' he said anxiously.

'Not a finger,' she reassured him. 'I think that he was more scared than I was in the end.' A thought occurred to her. 'How come you were there?'

He smiled. 'After Alistair had rung the police he had me tannoyed—thought I'd want to be there.'

'You mean he knew about us?'

'It seems that the whole hospital knows about "us",' he answered wryly. 'We've obviously been transparently displaying all the signs of being in love!'

She felt all reason leave her body as he started to kiss her, his hand moving to the thin material of her shirt.

'Too many buttons,' he complained, his fingers sending ripples of pleasure down the warm softness of her skin.

He made love to her as if they had been apart months, not days, and the spoken acknowledgement of that love gave their caresses new meaning, so that the physical act became more intense, more moving, and more fulfilling than she would ever have believed possible.

They lay together facing one another afterwards, close together on the small sofa, exchanging the gentle kisses of lovers, his fingers moving reverently across her face.

'Were you very frightened in there today?' he asked softly.

She thought for a moment, remembering how her initial terror at being manhandled into the office had dissolved into sympathy for him. 'I was at first,' she told him. 'But then I felt strangely detached.'

He kissed the tip of her nose, and she kissed him back. 'I've just been thinking.'

'Really?' he teased her. 'That's a new name for it!'

'No, really. Listen to me.'

'I'm listening.'

'In a way it was partly my fault that Mr Banks took it into his head to blame me for what had happened to his son, because I became over-involved in the case. You might even say that I interfered, although I would defend to the death my reasons for doing so. I want you to answer me something—not as my lover, but as my boss. Do you think I've got what it takes to be a good clinical doctor?'

He sat up and ran his fingers through his hair. 'That isn't a very fair question to ask me when I'm lying next to you half naked,' he objected smilingly.

'Don't prevaricate. Answer me.'

He ran his hand thoughtfully over the stubble which was beginning to appear on his jaw. 'Intellectually, I can't fault you—and you're an excellent diagnostician. . .'

'But?'

The incredible turquoise eyes were turned on her. 'I think you've hit the nail on the head yourself, Lu—you don't need me to tell you what you already know. I think that you *do* become over-involved with your patients, and I think that at some time in the future it could affect your clinical judgement.'

She had turned away from him, her shoulders shaking, and he grabbed her anxiously. 'You aren't crying, are you?'

'No, you fool,' she giggled up at him. 'Thank you, darling.'

He looked bewildered. 'For what?'

'For your impartiality. For treating me as an equal. I think I've known for some time that I'm never going to make it on the wards, and in a way it's going to be a blessing for us.'

'You're talking in riddles, Dr Gray!'

'Then stop interrupting and listen to me! If we both worked on the wards we wouldn't get very much time together, but if I started a career in biochemistry——'

'Biochemistry?'

'I won the biochemistry prize in med school,' she said demurely. 'It satisfies my diagnostic leanings, it gives me regular hours, *and* week-ends off. I've only one more house job to do. I'll go and see the Prof here tomorrow, see if he can fix me up. It will be very useful——' a secret smile '—if we decide to have a family.'

His face registered sheer delight. 'A family? Would you like to?'

She nodded. 'In a year or two I think I would, if you're agreed.'

For answer he kissed her pale shoulder, smoothing back a lock of the chestnut hair which lay over it and then she squealed as he picked her up and flung her over his shoulder, heading towards the bedroom door.

'Now where are we going?' she inquired innocently.

'Why, Dr Gray—you're going to show me exactly why you're the best pupil I've ever had!'

'Oh, Adam,' she sighed blissfully. 'You're insatiable!'

Mills & Boon

Medical Romances

4 MEDICAL ROMANCES & 2 GIFTS-FREE!

Capture all the excitement, intrigue and emotion of the busy world of medicine - by accepting four **FREE** Medical Romances, a pair of decorative glass oyster dishes and a special mystery gift.

Then, if you choose, go on to enjoy 6 more exciting Medical Romances every two months! Send the coupon below at once to **Reader Service, FREEPOST, P.O. Box 236, Croydon, Surrey CR9 9EL.**

✂-------------------- *No stamp required* --------

YES! Please rush me my **4 Free Medical Romances** and 2 Free Gifts! Please also reserve me a Reader Service Subscription. If I decide to subscribe, I can look forward to receiving 6 Medical Romances every two months, for just £8.10 delivered direct to my door. Post and packing is **free**, and there's a free Mills & Boon Newsletter. If I choose not to subscribe I shall write within 10 days - I can keep the books and gifts whatever I decide. I can cancel or suspend my subscription at any time, I am over18.

EP74D

NAME _____

ADDRESS _____

_____

_____ POSTCODE _____

SIGNATURE _____

COMPELLING FINAL CHAPTER

EDEN – Penny Richards   £2.99

The final novel in this sensational quartet tracing the lives of four very different sisters.
After helping her younger sisters to find love. Eden felt she'd missed her own chance of happiness. Then Nick Logan blew into her life like a breath of fresh air! His young good-looks threatened her respectable reputation – but if this was her one chance at love, Eden was determined to take it.

July 1990

W RLDWIDE

DREAM SONG TITLES COMPETITION
HOW TO ENTER

Listed below are 5 incomplete song titles. To enter simply choose the missing word from the selection of words listed and write it on the dotted line provided to complete each song title.

A. . . . . DREAMS   LOVER

B.   DAY DREAM . . . .   ELECTRIC

C.   DREAM . . . .   CHRISTMAS

D.   . . . . UPON A DREAM   BELIEVER

E.   I'M DREAMING OF A WHITE . . . .   ONCE

When you have completed each of the song titles, fill in the box below, placing the songs in an order ranging from the one you think is the most romantic, through to the one you think is the least romantic.

Use the letter corresponding to the song titles when filling in the five boxes. For example: If you think C. is the most romantic song, place the letter C. in the 1st box.

	1st	2nd	3rd	4th	5th
LETTER OF CHOSEN SONG					

MRS/MISS/MR . . . .

ADDRESS . . . .

. . . .

POSTCODE . . . . COUNTRY . . . .

CLOSING DATE: 31st DECEMBER, 1990

PLEASE SEND YOUR COMPLETED ENTRY TO EITHER:

Dream Book Offer, Eton House, 18-24 Paradise Road, Richmond, Surrey, ENGLAND TW9 1SR.

OR (Readers in Southern Africa)

Dream Book Offer, IBS Pty Ltd., Private Bag X3010, Randburg 2125, SOUTH AFRICA.

- Please retain this section.